ACE

ACE

*Arresting, Contemporary
stories by Emerging writers*

RECENT
WORK
PRESS

ACE: Arresting, Contemporary stories by Emerging writers
Recent Work Press
Canberra, Australia

ISBN: 9780648404217(paperback)

A catalogue record for this
book is available from the
National Library of Australia

Cover photograph: 'night' by Shuets Udono, 2006, reproduced under Creative
Commons attribution licence 2.0
Cover design: Recent Work Press
Set by Recent Work Press

recentworkpress.com

Australasian Association of Writing Programs

Contents

Gop Noi   1
Supatra Walker

Pigdog   6
Joshua Kemp

Song of Shadows   16
Andrew Drummond

Samuel   26
Alison Kelly

Finally, Our Feet Go Where They Want   35
Sue Brennan

All the Lives I Might Have Lived   42
Ivana Rnjak

Coffee and Copper   48
Sophie MacNeill

Paper Cranes   58
Ruth Armstrong

Countdown to New Year   69
Kerrie Knox

A Shift   77
Lisa Smithies

Afterword: Capturing the Unsayable   86
Julia Prendergast

Acknowledgements   98

Biographies   99

Gop Noi

Supatra Walker

I ball together a few grains of sticky rice from the little bamboo basket. Pinching a small piece of omelette from the tin plate on the floor in front of me, I press it into the rice. I place the ball of food in my mouth, chewing carefully, making sure that the mixture is fine and moist. In the hollow of my *pak toong* he lies quietly, studying my face. His eyes are as black as *lumyai* seeds. He slips an arm from the loose cotton wrap and it twitches intermittently against my knee. Satisfied that the food is thoroughly chewed, I spit some onto my fingers and gently push it into his soft mouth. He jerks in response. He sucks and blows noisily, like the mouths of the orange carp in the temple ponds. His eyes widen with surprise as he thrashes, food and saliva dribble from his lips. I scoop the slushy mash back into his mouth.

'*Gin, gin nah luk,* eat, eat my child,' I encourage him gently.

He sucks my finger thoughtfully, greedily. His face is serious. He has my mother's eyes. She would have loved him. If she were alive, she would have loved him. But then he wouldn't be here: she would never have consented to any of it. He smacks his lips noisily. His limbs jerk. He likes the food. There is a faint tug in my breasts but I have nothing for him. I make another ball of food and as I chew, I stroke his legs. He gurgles and wriggles, his movements strong but uncoordinated. In my lap he reminds me of a paddy frog. His long limbs—thin little thighs. Gop, that's what I call him. *Gop noi*, my little frog. I will give him another mouthful of food and then no more tonight. There is a bottle of warm milk ready for him. He will sleep beside me on the small kapok mattress on the floor of this room that contains the sum of my life.

I rent this room from *Mae* Buah. She too is from Isaan, from the same town as my mother. We are *luk pee luk nong*, cousins on my mother's side, although she is very much older than me. She has lived here in Bangkok since before I was born. There is another girl who lives in this house. Ped is older than me, maybe nineteen or twenty. Her baby is American. Like me she is from Isaan but she pretends she is from Chieng Mai. Her skin is whiter than mine so people believe her. She works in the best department store in Bangkok. She wears sunglasses, American, like all the movie stars wear, like the eyes of cats. She thinks she looks like Elizabeth Taylor. She has a new boyfriend and, increasingly, she leaves her son with Mae Buah at night. Mae Buah already cares for two other children. I don't know who their mothers are or where they live but they too are from the Northeast. They pay Mae Buah to look after their children. Just like I do. When I come home from my job I help Mae Buah bathe and feed the children. At times, they all share a mattress on the floor of her room. When I go to my job six days a week, Mae Buah looks after my son. I make just enough money to pay my rent and for food, and for my baby's milk and his care. If I am careful and can save a few baht I will go to the movies with Ped. But I am saving for a pair of sunglasses.

At my job I look after two children, a boy and a younger girl whose parents work at the same store as Ped. They go to work very early in the morning. I wake the children, feed them and walk them to school along the *klong*. Then I go back to the house where I will sweep the yard, wash the clothes and clean the house and kitchen. In the afternoons I fetch the children from school. At about four o'clock, Jim comes home from university and takes care of his sister's children so I can go home. He is a nice boy with a kind smile and he often teases me about my red hair. He has ambitions and is studying to be an engineer. He tells me that I should do a typing course and that maybe I will find work in an office: 'A pretty girl like you who can read and write English will be in big demand,' he says. He knows a woman who works in the typing pool at the Coca Cola factory. I haven't thought about my future since my son was born. He wasn't meant to be part of it, but the life of my dreams and that of my reality parted when my mother died.

I look down at my son and lightly pinch his soft thighs. There is some fat on him now. Not like in those first few weeks. He got sick. His diarrhoea was hot and yellow, like his face, and his little belly swelled like a bullfrog. I took him back to the hospital. They made me leave him there and sent me home. Every morning, with full breasts I would catch buses through the city's noisy diesel-fumed throng, to the hospital where I would spend the day. I fed and cared for him in that big hospital with its wide rooms, the crowded corridors and everywhere the sound of children crying. After a week the brusque doctor said he was well enough to go home. I hadn't brought in any clothes. It was hot. My baby had nothing but the hospital diaper he wore.

'Take off his diaper and leave it in the cot. The orderlies will clean up,' said the Thai nurse in her starched white cap and white uniform and white shoes. Her skin was pale, like milk. Her eyes were brown like *nam dan oi*, the golden sugar made from sugar cane—the eyes of privilege. She did not smile. Her lips were pursed like *dtood maa*, a dog's arse.

'I have no clothes for him,' I said. 'No blanket, not even a *pakama* in which to wrap him.'

'This is a hospital,' she said stiffly. 'This is not a charity.'

I did as she instructed. Then I picked up my naked son and, holding him against my chest, I turned and walked from the cot. I felt her eyes on my back. Through them I saw the sallowness of my Audrey Hepburn blouse, white, with the Peter Pan collar. I bought it from the expensive department store, laying out the creased, carefully saved baht notes on the polished counter. I felt the thinness of my *pak toong*. How faded its once bright patterns. I heard my rubber thongs as they slapped across the sanitised tiled floor. I saw the deep cracks in my heels stained with dirt that no amount of scrubbing would remove. And I saw the darkness of my skin. Northern black, skin like mud. I felt the coarseness of my hair, like the dry fibres of coconut husks and, as I walked out into the Bangkok afternoon with its trams and *tuk-tuks* and the buses and their horns and the merciless April sun, I looked down and saw the trails of salt glistening on my baby's back where my tears were drying.

Against my will and because of my sadness a memory begins to form—of clouds gathering, towering. Stiffening winds gust across dry, salt-panned rice fields, sweeping up the rice chaff and the stubble of last season's harvest. Driving gales shred the mango trees, sending their hard green fruit crashing on to the sun-baked, bone-dry mud, splitting the sour flesh from the soft white seeds. Tall coconut palms thrash, bowing to the drums of rolling thunder, while lightning gilds the boiling clouds, hurling heavy drops of rain in fierce, dense curtains across the plateau. When the storms are spent and the world grows quiet, the first tentative call of the paddy frog can be heard. *Gop Na*, whirring, churring, creaking and croaking. First one, then another, and then more until the once-dry paddy fields ring and pulse with the joy of frogs emerging from thick mud. Northern mud, rich and black, into which my family will plant soft stalks of seedling rice. Soon catfish and eels, crabs, snails and shrimp will thrive amongst the emerald spears. *Nai naam mee bplaa nai naa mee khao.* In the water there is fish, in the field there is rice.

In the bus shelter someone has left a newspaper, discarded on the dusty concrete along with the split watermelon seeds and steamed banana leaf wrappers that once held *khao tom mat,* sweet coconut rice with banana filling. Holding my son in one arm I gather up the papers and place them neatly back down on the concrete. I lay my baby on the papers and wrap him the way I was taught to wrap food in banana leaf. I board a bus with my son in his newspaper parcel and return to the *soi* where we live.

Under the harsh light of the naked bulb hanging from the ceiling, he squirms. *Gop noi, gop na*, little frog, paddy frog, far from home. I pick up my son and cover his taut little belly with kisses. He squeals. My laughter startles him and he kicks and throws up his arms. I put my ear to his chest and I can hear the tap tap tap of his little heart. I feel it beating lightly against my cheek like the rhythmic pulsing of a paddy frog's throat and an intense joy wells within me. I put my lips to his belly and I suck and suck and inhale his scent with deep, full breaths.

Pigdog

Joshua Kemp

I meet her in the forest. A place you wouldn't necessarily think you'd just bump into someone. She tells me she's not lost but I don't believe her.

She should be uncomfortable, stuck out here on her own with a strange guy. I'm aware of this as we start in the same direction, surrounded by karri forest in a wilderness area the size of a European country. I'm always aware of this when I'm out hiking and I run into a girl alone, or even a group of girls. There's a flash of caution in their eyes, the look of a grey roo on the roadside, about to cross the highway. But not this girl, there's no fear in her at all. Maybe it's because she's a couple of years older than me. A foot taller, slightly muscly. Looks like she could overpower me, so there's no need for her to be afraid. She talks like she knows more, or thinks she knows more than me.

By the time I lead her to the safety of the camping area she's basically told me her life story. She's from Byron Bay, moved West to visit friends. She was working at a restaurant in Busselton when she heard about the Bibbulmun Track, and decided on a whim to do it. We unload our gear and set up our tents and by the time night's fallen I realise I've hardly got a word in. That she hasn't asked a single thing about me in return.

I tell her I'm tired and wish her a good night's sleep, dropping exhaustedly onto my flimsy hiker's mattress. Only then I lay there with my heart burning like the fire I can see through the tent wall. Shapeless like a red ghost. Ashamed because I want to shut my eyes and hear her tugging at the zipper on my tent door.

Then I hear her douse the fire with water from the camp kettle. The steaming hiss. The zip on her tent before she clambers in the dark.

In the morning we part ways. I'm going to Mount Pingerup and she's heading for Pemberton. She tells me she'll only be in the timber town for a month or so before heading back toward Walpole. She says we should catch up. She gives me her number on a piece of paper torn out of her journal because our phones aren't working.

We're complete strangers. We've known each other less than twenty-four hours and yet she moves in to give me a hug before leaving. I have no idea what's going on. Her arms are open only a little but I step away and look at the ground. Her eyes fog over with confusion and she takes a step back as well.

We wave and sing out goodbye under the karris but it's awkward now. As I watch her disappear, I realise I don't even know her name.

The past six months I feel like I've been in freefall. Half a year I've been waiting to see when I'd hit the ground.

Last week I hit the unforgiving footpath outside the Ship. The ground seemed to rise up at me as if I was in a dream, outside of myself. My face bounced off the pavers and I felt nothing at first but then I saw the blood. Other bodies were dropping around me, thwacking on the concrete, and punches coming from all directions. Someone landed on top of me as I reached into my mouth and pulled a tooth clear. They wriggled and fought. Everyone looked at me in shock when I started screaming. A grown man wailing like a baby.

It's only a week later and my face is still aching with the hurt, but my pride took most of the battering. I can still see Wayno's confused face, tightening into a sly grin, when I started to shriek. I reach up now and feel my swollen cheek, the dull throb of pain when I press against it. I imagine it's the same colour as the cloud hugging the forest-tops. That glum dark blue. I can't see the mountain from here as it's blanketed with karris, salmon-coloured trees draped in hanging bark. Ahead I can hear the white-tailed black cockatoos singing, their mournful, throaty shrieks. I've been hearing them the past six months. The mountain, calling me.

The jarrah woodlands fall back and suddenly the path steepens through three-headed balgas and hairy sheoaks, so thick I can barely see a metre through them. I replay the awkward near-hug over and over in my head but it seems pretty trivial now. The morning rain has left everything dripping and green like a child's dream of a Christmas forest.

Soon I'm hunkered, panting, and peering up at the biggest karri I've ever seen. So tall it pierces the dark canopy and lets in a little iron light. It's bark-strapping all peeled and rotting around its roots.

This is the clearest I'll ever know myself, I realise. In the forest, alone. It's like there's a camera lens in the sky, and it's fixing in on me. Everything's real and I know every particle of myself clear as the drops of rain that trickle from the sheoaks.

Then I see them. Upright shadows, walking. Faceless blackfellas who emerge soundlessly from behind the giant karri. But they're only men for a moment, and then they're something else. Now they're four dogs. Blotched different colours and picking around the gnarly roots, sniffing the air the way I remember them doing.

My dad's pigdogs. Dead ten years but here they are now. Still watching out for me and stiffening to track their prey in the tree-line.

I blink and they're gone. I'm trembling so hard I can hear my jaw chattering, anxiously tonguing at the gum where that tooth popped out last week.

I should be dead. My head hitting the footpath like that. But I knew I was being looked after. The whole time I was pitched outside of myself, held at a distance from what was happening. Coddled in some warm fuzz just beyond the falling bodies and blood. I could take a blow like that and come out of it fine. Maybe that's why I wasn't worried about being in freefall all this time. Because I knew the pigdogs would be there, forming their protective circle.

Suddenly the voice of the mountain is screaming. I peer into the tops of the mammoth karri, a flock of black cockatoos is clambering along its tallest boughs. They're cranky shits and squawk at each other. It takes a moment for me to realise fruit and jags of bark are falling at my feet. Thwacking the ground hard. The cockies are tearing at the tree and their debris is raining down.

I move now, just in case something falls on me. Some of those big karri boughs can just fall at any time and crush unknowing hikers to death. But I know the pigdogs are here, somewhere or all around me. A shard of bark spins through the air and lands directly at my feet, slicing into the mire like a dropped knife. I'm laughing in disbelief and staying right where I am. Because I know nothing's going to hit me, touch me. The cockies rip and tear and everything's dropping.

Under the dark, twisted canopy, not even the rain can reach me.

The lights of my hometown look less imposing when I'm standing among the trees. Walpole's as sleepy as ever. Some wood smoke corkscrews from a chimney and, on the corner, is Aunt Sheridan's motel. Across the road, the wilderness takes hold again. It tangles and twists, awash in honey-blood blossoms. The dark is so inviting, calls to something primal inside, and always has. When I was a kid we used to drive past these same ageless trees and I'd watch the way they'd fall out of the light. Me in the back with the pigdogs. Their humid breath filling my sickly, wheezing lungs.

I go inside and wait at reception. Elvis from the stereo. I'm spinning on the spot. Aunt Sheridan steps out of the kitchen. Her eyes wash over me without a glint of recognition, like I'm just another motel guest. Her back is more crooked than I remember, humped. Making her look more ghastly than ever, hunched and limping, dragging the damaged leg she acquired as a little girl. An accident involving an overturned tractor.

No pleasantries. Her gauzy eyes drink me in but hardly register me. 'Need a room?'

'If that's okay?'

'Have to work for it. Not a charity. Charity's what killed ya dad so early.'

'I'll work, Aunty. Thanks.'

She's already flicking through the keys on their pins on the wall. 'Can take over the bar. Stella's gettin' sick of it.'

Her name cuts through my guts like I'm made of half-melted butter. I'm scared and screaming, pinned to the wet dirt again. A child pissing his pants.

'It'll be good to see her,' I say.

The room's pretty close to the kitchen so it smells of pig fat and coriander. Aunt Sheridan limps back toward reception and I watch her spidery shadow eat up the peeling wallpaper. I close my eyes above the bed and hold Mount Pingerup inside. Its black, karri-peppered skin within my own. It's the only thing holding me in place.

I start work the next night in a freshly-ironed, collared shirt smelling of frangipani. Aunt Sheridan insisted I wear it, pressed it on me with her bunion-fucked fingers. When I step into the restaurant Stella is standing in her apron watching the footy game on telly. Seeing her from behind, her plaited blond hair, I feel nothing. No terror as I expected. She's just a person. My beautiful, aloof cousin.

'Long time,' I say.

She glances at me. 'Heard you were back. Sick'a Busso?'

'Aw ya know. We've all gotta come home sometime, don't we?'

She smirks bitterly. 'Some of us never leave.'

She looks a little different. She has a crappy, rose tattoo on one shoulder, which I can tell she regrets because she keeps trying to cover it up. She launches into a chesty, hacking cough every now and then, from ciggies and the pot. Aunt Sheridan tells me she had a mean boyfriend for a while. She never says it outright, but hints there might've been a beating or two.

The restaurant work is easy. We're lucky to get three or four tables filled a night. A few more on the weekends. Stella and I hardly ever talk. When we're not cleaning glasses or setting out cutlery, we watch the telly. Sometimes standing beside each other. I like the proximity, but she gives off no warmth. I can separate this person from the child I remember out on the farm, when the cousins used to visit and run amok. People grow up. Sometimes they get meaner. And some, like Stella, just turn cold.

My days are completely free. I drive out to the farm every now and then just to look around. The house looks exactly the same as I remember, out behind the paddock, but another family lives here now. I get out and saunter down the firebreak and stand at the forest-edge and imagine the howls of the pigdogs. Different to the call of Mount Pingerup. Much sadder than the call of the mountain.

My cousins used to come out on weekends. Stella and her two brothers, Meek and Ellis. They were mean little shits. They'd kick the cows up their arses with their gumboots. Start small fires with stolen Zippos.

They were playing hopscotch out the back one time and I got pissed off at being excluded, which wasn't unusual. I started stepping in the way, joining in without being invited. Their rage was so rewarding, I started to laugh. They chased me through the paddock, laughing themselves. For the first time I felt like they were letting me in, accepting. All that time, the only thing I had to do was be as annoying and nasty as they were.

Vaulting over the fence, I pressed into the firebreak, and that's where Ellis tripped me up. The brothers pinned me to the dirt, still laughing into my face. And I was giggling back, but the giggle was dying. Stella joined in too, holding me down.

'Okay, okay. I'm sorry. Let me up now.'

Looking back at it now, I would've thought kids would know. Surely, they knew when enough was enough.

The three of them piled on top of me. Stella directly above, her two brothers on top of her. A squirming tangle of children fitting in the firebreak. They knew the problems I'd had when I was little. The asthma attacks in the middle of the night. Months in hospital, hooked up to nebulisers.

I couldn't breathe. My sickly lungs convulsed. I was screaming for them to let me go.

But Stella just laughed. She pivoted so her arse was in my face, suffocating me. And then not her arse. And the smell hit me. Something clammy. Meaty. The wet heat stifling my breath. Choking the air out of me until the forest started to darken and I passed out.

I think about the girl on the Bibbulmun Track a lot, the girl whose name I never asked for. I even go to the visitors centre and grab a pamphlet about the track. I try counting the days it would take her to get from Pemberton to here, imagining how I could just happen to run into her again somewhere along the way. Standing at the bar, listening to Sinatra croon sadly, I imagine her walking into the motel one night, her eyes brightening when she sees me.

The nights pick up as the April school holidays start. We've got about six or seven full tables instead of three or four. Stella and I work around each other at the beer taps, at the till. Sometimes we bump or touch but we never say anything.

I begin to like the routine at night. People dribbling in. Watching Aunt Sheridan limp between the tables. The sad old songs. Stella's plaited hair bumping against her back. Watching the red-flowering gum just outside the window and the way headlights swing across it and make it shiny and pale as moonlight, ghostly. When I see this I'm a kid again, in the back of dad's car with the pigdogs. I can breathe the darkness out of the trees.

After work I laze around in bed and go over my brief encounter with the girl on the Bibbulmun Track obsessively. Sometimes curling up with embarrassment at something stupid I said, or my awkwardness when she tried to hug me. Ashamed at how I waited in my tent that night, waiting for her to pull the zipper down and come in. How pathetic that was. To expect that from a stranger.

Somehow I'm not surprised the night my door handle turns

and I sit up in bed to watch Stella creep through the darkness. She doesn't say anything and I know this is all about her. Hands flat on my chest like she's holding me down in the firebreak again, only I can breathe this time.

She looks pissed off when I come, making soft, whining noises. But then she turns aloof as normal, wipes me with the blanket and just waits for me to get hard again.

She leaves, a pale banshee in midnight dark, and I don't see her again until the following night in the restaurant. We step around each other to get to the till. Pour Cokes and beer and carry out the steak sandwiches.

That weekend I drive out to Mount Frankland for a hike and take the Caldyanup Trail through the skinned bodies of the karris. I like to think I might run into the girl somewhere along here, somewhere along her travels, on her way back from Pemberton.

Instead all I can think about is Stella, sneaking into my room. The idea of her falling pregnant scares the hell out of me. The idea of becoming a father has always scared me shitless, but this is different. We're cousins. She might not believe in abortion, she might want to keep the thing. It would come out all wrong. Misshapen and weird. That's what happens when cousins or siblings fuck.

It would be born strange. Everyone would see. Everyone would know.

I try to shake these thoughts with the sheer side of the black mountain right next to me. But in the forest all around, I can hear the sounds of children. Two kids running ahead of me. Hooded figures in their rain jackets, skipping through the vivid karri hazel, yapping, making dog sounds.

I'd forgotten it is school holidays. The last weekend, thank Christ.

The kids' parents are just ahead on the trail, so tiny beneath Mount Frankland in the grey sky and the partly shed karri skins. I pass the parents and smile widely just to let them know I'm not Ivan Milat. They nod back and let me through.

It's a boy and a girl. Blonde and pale as spilt milk on a dark floor. The black mountain towers.

'Hey, you kids!' the father calls out. 'Wait for us please!'

Obedient children. They stop to let me through. The boy yaps and his voice echoes through the forest.

'What are you s'posed to be?' I ask as I weave between them.

He just frowns. 'A dog. Silly.'

'But you have to be careful when you call wild dogs,' the little girl tells her brother matter-of-factly. 'Coz they might follow you home.'

I smile and pass the boy. The girl runs ahead in front of me and now I'm closer I see her smile drop. Her eyes cast to the forest floor.

I remember the boars running through the karri hazel, their stink. Cold sweat and hot breath intermingling. And now I'm shivering and light, like I've had too much sugar. The big iris in the sky fixing on me. I put my nose to the air, the way the pigdogs used to when they caught the scent of something in the tree-line, sniffing the air before bringing the pigs down and opening them up. Red guts steaming in the morning light like karri mist.

Further down the trail I'm snatching for breath. Behind me the kids run ahead of their parents again. I can hear them coming after me, giving chase. Barking and yapping. Howling now. Wild dogs racing through the forest.

Following me home.

Song of Shadows

Andrew Drummond

Verse One, line 4: Angin midit mangidul

Josh comes back into the apartment, lays the second letter on the carpet, gives the hand-delivered envelope to Kate. It is made of good stock, thick and cream-coloured, sealed with a bow of ribbon.

Kate unties the ribbon and folds open the envelope.

'It's an invitation,' she says, holding it up for Josh to see.

The heading is in dark brown ink with gold shadowing—penned by hand.

It's for the birth,' Kate says.

Really?' Josh says.

Kate says, 'In Bali. Can you believe it?'

Are you serious?'

Yes.'

Hell,' Josh says. 'Overseas weddings, okay. But this.'

'What's next?' Kate says. 'Pet birthdays?'

Their laughter does not fill the room. It is small and edged with something else. The other letter is from The Clinic.

Verse Two, line 1: Yekti sangkan paraning dumadi

A bright young nurse comes into the waiting area, smiles at them with familiarity. Kate and Josh move to her. The nurse points Josh along a corridor and to the right, even though he knows the way. Each of the previous tests has been clear—for both of them.

Kate stays with the nurse, who shepherds her into a treatment room, stark and white. 'Are you ok?' the nurse asks after she has adjusted the stirrups and opened Kate's gown.

'Is there a fan on?' Kate says. 'I can feel a breeze.'

The nurse smiles. 'He'll be here in a minute.'

Kate breathes in slowly and deeply, allows air to fill her lungs and soak her body with oxygen. The room is so quiet, the hum of electrical equipment has become audible. Kate thinks on this hum. It was always there, beneath the surface noise. Kate thinks, it's only when things have settled that this world becomes one.

The radiologist comes into the room, is nice enough, injects the dye and makes sure Kate is comfortable. Kate says she is, feeling the viscous cold ooze through her like mercury through a thermometer. This is how she imagines it.

After the radiologist has left the room and taken the images, Kate is allowed to clean herself and get dressed. Josh is reading in the waiting area. He looks up when Kate comes out.

Verse Two, line 2: Surya Candra kalawan Kartika

It is late—working back again—when he gets to the final set of images. Moonlight filters through his office window, gently highlighting the framed degrees that line his wall more out of obligation than pride.

He clips an image to the lightbox. As soon as he sees the shadow, he knows.

Proximal occlusion.

The matter is decided as simply and quickly as this—the time it takes to think two words.

It is now his knowledge. The couple made it clear they did not want to know who or what or why. 'We don't want that cloud,' they said. And so he must rest with it, lie with it, know this thing about the world, carry his burden.

As always.

It is impossible to sit in his position and not speculate. He is intimate with the calling cards of trauma and infection. With a proximal, a septic most often follows. So many of the women he sees—usually when they were young, before they were married or with the partner sitting nervously in the waiting area. A lot of hack jobs, if he is speaking honestly. Cut and shuts. Sometimes they get away with it. Other times, the damage is too great.

He looks again at the image on the lightbox. Yes, it is his burden. He will never know the truth about this woman, this life. He turns away and notices the moonlight on his degrees. This is what they have brought.

Verse One, line 9: Sayekti nandhang prihatin

Things have settled like sediment at the bottom of a river.

'Do you want to go?' Kate says.

'I'm not sure.'

'I could use a break,' Kate says, 'from work.'

'It'll be relaxing,' Josh says.

Kate remembers something from long before Josh. She pauses in her thoughts. Rain continues to drum against the roof. Kate breathes in and slightly opens her mouth, as if to speak. Josh looks at her in anticipation of what is to come.

Kate says nothing, closes her mouth.

Verse One, line 9: Neng pondhokan sayekti

Flying in a blue sky, jetting above the white pillow clouds with everything so small below. Sensing the slow movement of the earth, rather than seeing it. Kate says, 'It's hard to believe people live down there.'

When they arc over the ocean and land at Ngurah Rai, their driver is waiting. His name is Slamet. He drives quickly along the sheeny streets, pulls the car onto the shoulder of the road in a place that seems empty.

'It's too small,' he says, pointing at a narrow alleyway. 'You'll need to walk. One kilometre.'

The sun drills into them. Josh stops and wriggles from his backpack, takes out a t-shirt and drapes it over his head, closes his backpack and heaves it up onto his shoulders again. Lines of sweat become rivers, the humidity a presence, an entity.

Finally they come to the hotel, an oasis of shade, and check in.

Kate studies the graceful movements of the woman at reception. 'I am Ni Man Dewi,' she says. 'Please let me know if you need anything.'

Verse Two, line 10: Gantha gatraning gesang

Kate sips tea while she waits for Slamet to pack the car. When all is ready, they drive into the hills, a new world of lush green jungle vegetation and rice paddies.

Ni Man Dewi's family is gracious—they welcome Kate with sembahs and dignified smiles.

Everyone moves to the paon, the kitchen, to begin class, cooking furiously all morning. Kate wonders if she will remember a thing.

After the soup broth is simmering and the baby carrots cut, Ni Man Dewi points at Kate's belly and says something in local language. The whole family laughs. Ni Man Dewi is confused by the hurt look on Kate's face as she glances down.

'You cook with Brahma,' Ni Man Dewi says, touching Kate's shoulder. 'God of Fire. He is in you today.'

When class is over, Ni Man Dewi and Kate stand in the street, waiting for Slamet to arrive. Kate notices a plaque on the compound gates. 'What's that?' she asks.

'That is my family,' Ni Man Dewi says. 'A list of their names.'

'Where are you?'

'Here,' Ni Man Dewi says, pointing out her name.

'It's a long list,' Kate says, smiling.

'It is getting longer,' Ni Man Dewi says, sweeping her hand across the bottom of the plaque. 'All of these are children.'

For some reason, Kate flinches. She composes herself and says, 'Your family is very lucky.'

Ni Man Dewi does not speak for a moment. She moves beside Kate and comes close to hugging her, puts one arm on her shoulder and rests the other on her belly. 'Majemak tunggal,' she says. 'Even though it is only in the form of a shadow, the universe also exists in human beings.'

Verse Two, lines 6-7: Bumi miwah dahana maruta lan banyu

Back at the hotel, Josh has left a note in the bungalow, gone to the beach. Kate dozes briefly, then wanders the grounds. By the time she reaches the place where Ni Man Dewi works, banten cover the floor like leaves in a courtyard. Ni Man Dewi motions to the tiles with her head, and Kate sits down.

Canang,' Ni Man Dewi says, holding up a palm-leaf basket. 'Ca— beautiful. Nang—purpose.'

As Ni Man Dewi constructs the offering, she explains each part, reveals each symbol. When the peporosan is complete, she outlines the Trimurti. She points out the gambier and the vividly red, south-facing flowers. She says, 'This is you. Brahma.'

Ni Man Dewi puts on her sarong and sash, asks Kate to join her slow walk around the hotel. Before they begin, Ni Man Dewi adds the crinkled banknotes, lights the incense, dips a jepun into the holy tirta and sprinkles some of this water over each banten. She says, 'It is complete. This is the fusion of earth, fire, wind and water.'

At the final stop on their walk, after she has secured the offering to Sang Hyang Widhi Wasa, Ni Man Dewi holds a palm facedown, waves three times and says a prayer. She looks to Kate and says, 'Sari is the essence. Smoke carries sari to God. We thank God for peace.'

'It's beautiful,' Kate says.

'It is not for us,' Ni Man Dewi says. 'Our time and effort is our sacrifice. We make them, give them, leave them for the unseen. That is their beautiful purpose. The world is self-filled. Our act is selfless.'

Kate says, 'You've given me gifts today.'

'This is our life,' Ni Man Dewi says, smiling.

Verse One, line 10: Dhuh nyawa gondhelana

Rain pounds the car. At one point, Slamet flicks the windscreen wipers to their top setting. 'No faster,' he says.

'No, faster,' Josh repeats, although he is talking about the accelerator.

The weight of rain is something Kate and Josh have learned in Bali, the way it can blanket. Slamet is accustomed. It is natural for him to drive these slick roads and not slow down.

For all its pounding, the rain is over by the time the car peaks in Ubud, a gentle trickling in the deep gutters the only sign it has rained at all. Slamet carries their bags this time, his thongs slapping against the wet ground.

In the evening, Kate and Josh meet Emma and Deene for dinner. Emma looks exhausted, and at the same time, filled with a radiant light.

'We've thought about it a lot,' she says, a slightly nervous strain in her voice, 'and we'd like you to be godparents.'

Emma is looking at Kate as she speaks. So is Deene.

Verse Two, line 9: Lahir batin wus kacakup dadi sawiji

The day before the birth, Kate and Josh witness a funeral procession. Sitting in the second storey of an internet café, they first hear the deep bass notes of the gamelan musicians, then the high tinkles.

Josh says, 'Come on. Let's go down to the street.'

The Wadah is beautiful, gilt at every level, highlighted by patterns of white and gold. Right up the tower, on every corner, flowers bobble from the ends of long wires.

Men carry the Wadah on their shoulders, meandering along the street from side to side, laughing and shouting. They rock the Wadah back and forth, the gathered crowd cheering and singing with joy. Other men fight to take possession of the tower, or run around in circles ahead of the gamelan musicians, who clang their instruments in orchestra.

As the procession, with all its colour and flowers and life, continues down the street, Kate notices a straggle of men dancing, joyous in their black and white cheque sarongs and batik udengs. Women follow close behind, colourful offerings held in trays or on their heads.

'Eat well tonight,' says the tourist standing next to Josh. 'They'll feast after the cremation, so why don't we? Fire might free the spirit and cleanse the soul, but only dinner can feed the body.'

The tourist laughs. Josh smiles politely.

Quietly under her breath, Kate says, 'Brahma.'

Verse One, line 3: Thenguk thenguk lungguh dhewe

That night, Kate and Josh sit on the cool tiles, drinking es teh, iced tea. It is quiet. Josh is reading Belloc, researching an essay.

Kate says, 'How was that procession?'

'Funny you say that,' Josh says. 'I was just thinking about it while I read this poem.'

He marks his book and reads to Kate:

Loss, and Possession, Death and Life are one
There falls no shadow where there shines no sun.

Verse Two, line 4: Cahya katri wus kumpul

The morning Emma goes into labour, Kate and Josh get ready to go quickly, wait impatiently for their driver to arrive.

Kate takes a heavy breath.

'You ok?' Josh says.

Kate says, 'I think so.'

'Fine with it?'

'We both know why they asked. At first, I wasn't sure, but now I'm ok. I've changed.'

'Changed your mind?'

'Not just that,' Kate says. 'Something more.'

Verse Two, line 1: Yekti sangkan paraning dumadi

One of the staff brings more towels into the birthing suite. Emma breathes fast and shallow, contracting and opening at the same time. The midwife quietly reassures her, says something Kate cannot hear.

Emma turns toward the window, crouches on all fours. The staff member who brought the towels positions one on the rim of the birthing pool. Emma rests her forehead against this towel and angles her pelvis down. Kate takes in the view from the window, all that Emma is

missing. The deep green vegetation dropping down to the waterway, the distant green hills.

Life revealing itself inside and out.

Emma's baby is close now. The midwife speaks quietly once more and Emma rolls onto her back. Deene arcs his arms through the space below Emma's shoulders and rests them on either edge of the birthing pool. Emma flops her hands on top of Deene's and their fingers intertwine.

Noise increases and the baby's head appears. Emma pants and cries with effort. The baby comes out easily, floats in the warm water for a moment, cupped by the midwife. In this moment, everything is still. No breath from the baby, who is yet to feel air on its cheeks. No breath from Emma or Deene. Nothing from the midwife or staff. Kate's lungs at rest. A collective suspension of sound and movement.

Almost of time.

Samuel

Alison Kelly

My house is chafed with soft rot. The paint has peeled, and the heartwood is falling away in caseous lumps that don't splinter, even if you pick at them. Grandpa's flat is downstairs. He looks small inside a stained shirt and waterproof parka. The newsreels illuminate his profile with blue light.

I iron clothes for twenty-five dollars per hamper. Steam rises from the clothes, releasing a plume of odors: the alkali tang of deodorants, starch, and cheap perfume resins. You can imagine the people that inhabit the clothes. There's a woman's shirt with a bank logo and I imagine her picking up her car keys and walking out the door to work. A man's shirt is paint-spattered. I imagine him laying down sheets and repainting his kitchen, barefoot on a stepladder. With each crease in the fabric I intrude into these bright and precious houses—doors that would never open for me in real life.

A man on the television has a whitetail stag in the cargo tray of his pickup and a twelve-gauge over his shoulder. His unarmed hand holds the velveteen crown of the stag's antlers aloft, to prove their span. The deer's eyes are black-glazed in a ventriloquist stupor.

'Never seen a deer in real life. Just a reindeer,' I say.

'Pests.' Grandpa shakes his head. 'Would come of a morning and eat all our roses.'

The water crackles in the iron. 'Never shot a gun. Not even an air rifle.'

Grandpa laughs and scratches behind his ear. 'I have. Automatic rifles, in the reserves. Too much recoil. None of us could shoot straight.' His teeth are the color of ivory dominoes. The gingivitis has stripped back his gum-line, making the teeth look particularly long. I wear a pit-stained cotton shirt, oversized jeans, and a pair of black underwear I took from my mother's closet. Grandpa has a fiscal ledger beside him. The left column bears the name of my dead Grandma, Barbara, and Joyce and Carol and all the others from her long-disbanded tennis club. The right column lists their imagined scores. Grandpa notes the results of these games for hours a day.

'I'm leaving,' I say.

Grandpa stares at me with dim alarm. 'Where you going?'

'Dinner. At Samuel's house.'

Grandpa raises his eyebrows. 'How long'll that take?'

'A few hours, probably.'

'When'll you be back?'

'In a few hours. I guess.' Even if I know an exact time, I can't tell him. He is trying to determine if he has enough time to call a taxi to Dan Murphy's and back for two bottles of scotch, then hide them behind the refrigerator before I arrive home.

But Grandpa seems satisfied with my answer. 'Well, that's good, isn't it? You need to make some friends.'

'I'll be quiet when I get back. I won't disturb you.'

Grandpa turns back to the television. 'I can sleep through

anything,' he says.

Samuel has broad arms from chopping lantana, and skin with a pale sheen like the underside of a shark. I have known him since I was twelve. At the end of Mum's eulogy, he strode out of eyeshot before the hearse reached the end of the funeral home's driveway. I asked for his number from Mum's work registrar. Now I shadow him around coffee-shops and beaches. Every so often he dispenses a cherished detail about Mum's working life—cigarette breaks outside the veterinary clinic, or work parties. Samuel doesn't work at mum's clinic anymore. He works at the reptile park, out in the back room—a bucket of live mice, to one side, and an empty bucket on the other. He picks up a mouse, snaps its neck, and drops it into the empty bucket. He does this until the empty bucket is full of dead mice.

That evening, I eat dinner with his family before he takes me to the spare-room in his parents' house. It contains two striped futons separated by a coffee table and a large flat-screen television.

'Haven't sat at the table for a family meal since I was a kid,' I tell him.

'I was thinking about that.' He smiles, cigarette nodding in his lips at each word.

Samuel owns a box full of crocodile teeth. They're from the banks of the Ganges—he sifted them from their shit. In India, you can even buy human teeth, he tells me, because the Indians are true entrepreneurs. He collects bones and teeth, but he doesn't hunt. He thinks it's so pointless, those rich people who pay to shoot lions from the back of cars, or poke rifles from the bars of cages. 'We should merge the prisons and the zoos and make a spectacle of it,' he says, 'like the Romans did'.

I sit up too quickly and hit my head on the window-ledge behind the lounge. He touches my head gently. I recoil at the awkwardness of his sudden affection, as if that gesture ignited some latent charge from each previously missed opportunity for contact, each cautiously passed teaspoon and coffee mug.

He looks at the white tally-marks of scar tissue on my arm.

I look away. 'Just cutting,' I say.

'You don't have to hide those from me, you know. Every woman I've been with has them.' He leans back and taps a cigarette out of his pack. 'I won't tell you it's wrong, and I won't tell you to stop. What difference would it make?' He stands up. 'That's my attitude towards things, anyway. You want a drink?'

'You drinkin'?' I ask.

'Nope. Thought you might want to.'

My cheeks are hot. 'No thanks, actually.'

'We got beer, red wine, white wine, whiskey.'

'I'm all good. I'm on Luvox. You know Eric Harris was on Luvox?'

'Eric Harris.' He closes the door to the hall.

'The Columbine guy.'

Samuel tells me about Roland Loomis' *Modern Primitives*. Today's youth are all lost because there are no rites of passage anymore. He shows me a sepia photograph depicting an expanse of wimpled scar-tissue, unfurling across the back of an aboriginal man. The man's expression is inscrutable, except for the jagged slant of his nose and outline of his thick eyelashes.

Samuel rolls up his pant-legs until they form a cuff above each knee. On each of his knees are pale white dots, the size of shoelace eyelets. 'This is where they hung me from,' he says. 'Suspension is the hanging of the body from titanium hooks,' he tells me. 'It made me feel weightless,' he adds.

Samuel goes to the bathroom and returns with his coarse beard shaved away. He yawns before he looks at his phone. 'Pretty late. Can crash here. If you want.'

I think of his mother. Maybe she will make me a cooked breakfast. 'If that's okay.'

'It is.'

'Saves you driving me home tonight,' I reason.

'That's right.'

'You shaved?'

He averts his eyes, strokes his jawline. 'Yes, I did,' he says, softly. He rarely looks at me directly.

I tell him about the night my grandmother died, and my mother slipped into my room at midnight. When she got into bed with me, her kimono and terrycloth bathrobe reeked of sweat and wine. She chanted 'My mum's dead,' and sobbed, then asked me to hold her. I pretended to be asleep.

I talk excitedly. It is good to be listened to. 'You know, I feel ugly all the time.' I tell him, laying on the lounge, arm over my head. 'You know how I see myself?'

'I don't think you're ugly,' he says. 'Not at all.'

Samuel decides he will sleep in this room, too. 'The paint smell, in my bedroom.' He wrinkles his nose, then asks, 'Have you ever been in a relationship before?'

'Guys just want to save me. I can read it in them.' Sometimes my voice gains this unfamiliar air of expertise, as if I actually know how men work. 'They get off on it, the helplessness.'

'You don't need to be saved.' A low urgency enters his voice. 'Tell me who you've been with. I might know them.'

I become frustrated. 'Why are asking me this stuff?'

'Would it be weird if I kissed you? Could I?'

'No,' I whisper, immediately.

'Do you mean 'No,' don't come over, or 'No,' it wouldn't be weird?'

I squint my eyes shut, my hands clenching into fists as they rest on my thighs. 'Okay. I mean, it wouldn't be weird.'

I don't look at him. As he moves towards me, the wire under the lounge upholstery creaks. His mouth is hot. Taste of ash. I hate the sound of him kissing me. I turn my face away.

'You wanna do this?' he asks me.

'Maybe not.' His proximity gives me a forced awareness of my own body. My palms are upturned and loose at my sides, 'Because of something bad happening to me when I was a kid.'

The weight of his chest meets me at each inward breath.

I can't breathe. 'I'm not right,' I say. 'No one can decide what's wrong—they've been trying since I was fifteen.'

He chuckles, his voice unexpectedly warm. 'I think you give yourself too much credit.'

He leans over me to switch off the lampshade. It becomes dark enough that opening or shutting my eyes doesn't make a difference. He takes off my shirt, shoes, socks, and my jeans. He peels my mother's underwear from my body. The mass of his torso is solid and square, pinning me to the lounge.

'Help me.' I don't shout this. I say it.

With his hands squeezing my arse, he says 'What?' Like he doesn't hear me. His erection is pressed against my thigh. He has decided this will happen and there is nothing I can do about it. Then I feel nothing. I turn my head and wait. Thin line of light under the door to the hallway.

Samuel drives me home when he's done.

'Didn't tell me you were a virgin,' he says.

'You didn't ask.'

'God. I did suspect.' He sighs. 'I'm older and I should've known better. You're not as honest as you think you are, you know.'

For a while there is silence, and the streetlight passes into the car in intervals, until I speak. 'What did I do wrong?'

'Think I'd rather just go home and sleep it off.'

I feel a hot surge of tears stinging my eyes. I blow my nose on the inside of my shirt. Cool mucus sticks to my chest. He will not see me cry. 'No jobs around here,' I say. 'Think I'll join the military.'

'You can't be a soldier, in the army. They don't treat women right.'

'Whatever. I didn't even mean it. They don't let people like me in.'

He looks at me out of the corner of his eye, then back at the road. 'You know. If you're okay with what happened tonight, then so am I.'

'Yeah.'

'It's not even a big deal.'

'Yes.'

'No need to tell everyone, right?'

'Right.'

I imagine a shotgun. I cradle the barrel with both hands on account of its heft and my weak arms. Samuel is kneeling in front of me, faced away, palms open in an attitude of surrender. His shadow falls in front of him because I am the source of light.

The car is humming in first gear, cruising around the terminus of an unfamiliar cul-de-sac. 'This isn't the way to my street. Where are you going?' I ask.

'I don't know,' Samuel replies, turning the car in a wide arc.

When I get home there's enough light outside to show that the windows are dirty, fine hairs and dust glowing on the panes. I eat seven peanut butter sandwiches. I indulge an impulse to curl up on the cool linoleum and listen to the living sounds of the house. Floorboards shrink and the fridge motor ticks into high gear. A thin film of awareness covers every curve of my body, like the slime of raw chicken.

I take a notebook and a blue ballpoint pen and write the exact details of the night in linear order, searching for an answer in the words. It seems to lie somewhere in the memory of Samuel's ugly mouth, the coarseness of the hair on his lower stomach, the mold of his eyelids around his downcast gaze. I slap myself in the face so hard that my ears ring.

As the ringing fades there's a hushed sound coming from Grandpa's floor, like the whistling friction of trouser legs. It turns out Grandpa is crawling up the stairs.

'Need help?'

'Nah, nah.' Grandpa's looks at the blue carpet on the steps then up at me in alarm, as if he is discovering my presence anew each time. He smells like scotch. I shouldn't have left him alone.

I grab his arm. I picture myself bending it gently, irreversibly in my grip. 'Stand up,' I say.

'Nah, nah, nah,' he says.

I give up and shepherd his crawl to the only accessible bed on this floor. It was Mum's recovery bed for after chemo sessions. He climbs on it and lies on his back. I tuck him in. In my irritation and need to avoid touching him, I fling the sheets too far. It covers his face like a burial shroud.

When he resurfaces, he clutches the sheets to his chin. 'Beautiful girl,' he says, and then winces, turns his face into the pillow and sobs.

I get on my bike, and ride down the main street. The young man across the road is standing in the yard with a garden-hose in his hand. The dawn rays light him up as I get close. There is no birdsong.

I remember his parents howling and the neighbours congregating outside their rusted fence, whispering, as if speculating on the progress of a housefire. He was only a boy then, toeing a worn soccer-ball from one side of the yard to the other with inconsolable lethargy.

The young man is slumped, gaze set firmly downward. I coast slowly now, pushing the brakes. He is directing the garden-hose at a square of turf, long churned-up. I stop. A clear stream of water roils the earth and makes mirror-faced pools in the divots.

Finally, Our Feet Go Where They Want

Sue Brennan

Once or twice a month, I pay, I mean, we pay... well, most often you pay, for nameless Chinese men to massage our feet. I like it medium pressure, you like it harder. I wonder if you're trying to prove something to me. Surely you are, sitting there on your mobile phone while a young man with strong hands grinds his knuckles into the balls of your feet. My guy is called Mr. X. Yours is Mr. M. We ... you call ahead and say we are coming and would prefer Mr. X and Mr. M if they are available. They know the pressure we want. We don't have to explain.

Before the massage, we eat at our favourite Indian place and you don't ask me how my morning at work was and I try and get information from you about yours: *What did you do? How many others were in today? Did you go out for coffee? Where?* I feel like an inquisitor, but you've forced me into this role. We climb the stairs after lunch, past the manga shop on the first floor above the covered, busy shopping street. We enter the dimly lit room and remove our shoes. You remove your shoes easily. Years, decades of practice—stepping on to the back of them and in to a pair of slippers. I still haven't quite got the hang of it. I need to be more mindful of my footwear choices. I lift each foot in front of me to unclip my shoes, stepping in to the over-sized slippers and shuffling over to where you are already paying for our session. I protest. *I can pay. I can pay.* It's useless.

There is pleasant, soothing, synthesised music playing and one other customer who, judging from the gaping mouth, is fast asleep. The masseur works on his feet regardless. Our guys are ready, so we take our positions side by side in the comfortable chairs and for the next forty minutes don't speak. I roll up the legs of my trousers to above my knees. You have a little more difficulty with your snug-fitting jeans. I have asked you why you are permitted to wear jeans to work—this is Japan after all—you said that on Saturdays you stay in the office, and don't meet with clients. It sounded reasonable back then.

A girl delivers basins of warm water, and I wait until Mr. X gestures for me to place my feet into one. They are washed briskly and then, my favourite part, each leg is wrapped in very warm towels. Mr. X wanders away out of sight and I lie there feeling coddled, pampered, and abandoned. I glance at you and you are equally swaddled, checking your phone as usual. I wonder what you'd do if I sent you a text. I look over at the other customer and squint to see what the masseur is showing the now-awake man. On a paper tissue are small, yellow chunks of skin. I gasp and look quickly away.

Mr. X returns bringing a small plastic seat, settles himself in front of me, sets the timer for 45 minutes and puts it on the floor. The blessed towels are removed and some kind of oil is smeared from knee to toe. I've given up caring much about my leg-stubble. I can't be constantly prepared for a massage and I didn't know that you were going to want to do this today. It's only a week since the last one. It starts with firm thumbs pressed slowly along my instep and a glance up at me for confirmation. I nod and smile. It's firm, on the edge of pleasure and *please stop*. How anyone could sleep through this is beyond me. I take furtive looks at Mr. X who is probably about twenty. All the men employed here look the same age. I wonder what he does in his free time. Perhaps he's a student and he hurries back to his apartment to finish an assignment. He checks that the towels aren't too hot. When he speaks to me it is in basic Japanese. *Daijoubu?* he asks. Is it alright? *Daijoubu*, I respond. Yes, it's alright.

The part I don't really like is the toes. I hope that he will hurry through or forget. He pushes into the base of each toe and I can deal with that, but when he pulls each toe firmly and releases them with a small snap of his fingers, I feel vaguely nauseated. He misses nothing. It's a routine; he could probably do it in his sleep. When one foot is done, it is wrapped in a warm, wet towel and put aside. Mr. M finishes with your left foot at almost the same time. We are halfway through and I can feel disappointment stirring. After this, we will go home on the bus, stopping at the supermarket to buy something for dinner. You will cook and I'll pretend to help. We've given up the idea that this would be a task equally shared. Simply, you're better at it than me. Not simply, I can't do it the way you want.

I go back to wondering about Mr. X. Does he have a girlfriend? A Japanese one? Surely yes, he's a good-looking young man. How I'd love to find out what he thinks of living here. What he thinks of *them*. I want us to sneak out the back where the basins and towels are kept and collude: *Do you feel like an outsider? Do you think I'd understand him better, I mean really know him, if I could speak better Japanese? Are Japanese women this ... remote?* I once had a Chinese student tell me that he had no friends here. *I'm lonely,* he said, *they don't talk to me.* Maybe that was just his story.

As Mr. X works away on my right foot, I know time is running out. I'd love to stay here for hours with him pressing the soles of my feet with his thumbs. There's nothing sexual in this; it is comforting and familiar rather than arousing or erotic. A few times, not recently, you have given me a massage. I remember the first time you offered to do this. I was excited and assumed it would lead to sex. You told me to lie on the bed and I did. You told me to keep my clothes on and I did. You told me to lie facedown and I adjusted the pillows so I wouldn't have my face squashed. You sat astride me. *Here we go*, I thought, and yes, off we went. It wasn't so much a massage as a pummel. Back in your university student days you were on the ice-hockey team and had sometimes acted as team masseur. Maybe you all took turns. As you kneaded the back of my thighs, I wanted to point out that I'd been teaching English to half-asleep freshmen, not whacking a puck around a rink and getting thrown into the barriers.

I look over at you and your eyes are closed and the phone is held against your chest like some kind of talisman. In front of the row of five chairs where we are seated are three private rooms. The facade is wooden with Chinese-inspired, carved lattice windows. Once, in the early days, I went there for a back massage and it was one of the girls who did it. You were out on the chair having your feet done. Now, I sit and watch a young man being ushered quietly into one of the rooms. The customer who was having his skin removed has disappeared—I didn't notice him leave—and a middle-aged woman is settling into position. This is a popular place, a well-known secret. They're always busy here and a few times Mr. X and Mr. M have not been available. That annoyed you more than me, to have to explain again the degree of pain you wanted to experience. To get exactly what you wanted.

Mr. X is pulling the toes on my right foot and I look over at your rectangular, blocky feet, wiry black tufts of hair on each toe and on top. You've told me you dislike them. To me all feet are ugly and I don't understand the fetishisation of them. As for shoes? Now there's something to worship. I look over at the collection of shoes at the entrance. We placed ours on a shelf, but the woman who just arrived left hers by the door. *We have a rebel in the house*, I think. The entrance of our apartment, the *genkan*, is neat. We bought and assembled a cupboard that holds most of our shoes and we have two pairs of slippers for guests, though we never wear them ourselves.

It's almost over now. Mr. X wraps my right foot in a warm damp towel and I lay there looking like a burn victim. He stands and, with the flat of his wide hands and the weight of his own body, he applies pressure from my knees and down to my feet. This is done twice and then I am lightly punched up and down the leg and on each sole. I feel he could go a little harder on this. A little bell rings; he's timed it perfectly. He peels the towels off and uses a fresh one to dry me before standing aside. *Arigato gozaimasu*, I say in a low voice and he nods. He gathers the towels and clock, without making eye contact, and leaves. Mr. M is also finishing up with you and I go over to the doorway, find our shoes and set them out. As you step into them and leave, I'm still fiddling around trying to do up the clip on the side. I can't quite see in the dimly lit room. When I come out on the small landing, you are stamping your feet into your shoes. I don't ask why you don't just do this inside before you go out.

We descend the narrow staircase and make our way to the bus stop. It's so crowded now that we walk one behind the other, no hand holding for us. My feet feel fat, tingly, and I wish that I could walk barefoot from the massage chair to our sofa and not through this shopping madness in high heels. All Mr. X's good work for nothing. Young couples meander, looking with equal interest at the window displays and their phones. Bent, old women push their wheeled shopping baskets with determination. Foreigners are also plentiful, looking for the small, quirky bars and cafes that make this trendy suburb of Tokyo so popular. Once we arrive at the bus stop and take our place in the queue, you complain about the crowds and reiterate that there should be a special walking lane for residents. You're only half-joking about this.

We're fourth and fifth in the queue and both checking our phones. There's a long email from my sister that I scroll through. I miss her keenly and decide to save it for later when I can drink a glass of wine, alone. I open an email from the university where I work. It says there will be medical examinations on campus in the forthcoming weeks and, as a full-time employee, I am expected to have yearly medicals. I look up to tell you about this and see the screen you are looking at—an email in Japanese punctuated with pink hearts and stars, a pair of clasping hands. You notice me looking, turn off the screen and slip the phone into your bag. The bus pulls up and we board. Usually, whichever one of us gets on first pays for the other. You board first, pay and I sit beside you meekly. Fuming.

We alight in front of the supermarket. Having planned dinner at lunch, we move around efficiently, putting the items we need in to a basket. At the register, I am ready with my wallet, as are you, and as soon as the last item is scanned, I whip some notes out and place them in the tray. I hear you exhale. We put the items into two plastic bags and you try to take both of them. I pull one from your hands. You close your eyes and when they open, I see the determination in them. We've fought this battle before. Outside you try again to take the bag and I say loudly, *I can carry it!* When you try yet again, I blurt, *Who was that email from?* You laugh and say it's from a co-worker. *A female co-worker?* I ask.

No, male.

I stand in the middle of the footpath staring at you. You nudge me to the side, pull your phone out of your bag and open the email. *Bit strange a guy using all those emojis,* I say. You explain, as if to a small child, what each one is for. The throbbing heart is because this co-worker is asking for a favour and the stars are because he is happy with your work. You turn the phone off and laugh again and explain that this is how Japanese people communicate with each other. I know you are lying—I know it, I know it, I know it—but I can't read Japanese well enough to prove it. We continue walking and you ask me what I want to do tomorrow. Do I want to go hiking?

Inside, we take our shoes off. You go ahead of me and into the kitchen. I remove mine slowly and squat to look for space inside the cupboard. On the bottom shelf is a pair of shoes I've only worn once. You bought them for me. On one of the rare occasions when I was out shopping by myself, I bought a black, patent leather, very nice pair of shoes. High heels and pointed toes. A little expensive. Two days later, you presented me with a pair of shoes that you said were identical for a fifth of the price. The only resemblance, as far as I could tell, was that they were a black pair of women's shoes. I was reminded of the nuns who taught me in high school: sexless in their Church-issued, sensible heels. When I put them on, I felt as though I aged forty years. I smiled and thanked you and said, *please don't buy me any more shoes, okay? I like shopping for them myself.*

When I leave you, they will be the first things I throw out.

All the Lives I Might Have Lived

Ivana Rnjak

It is early on a slow summer's Sunday morning and I am going a cool 80 on the highway, deep into Sydney's west. The sun is rising steadily up ahead as an old Serbian song wails through the speakers. With the window down, I can smell smoke and singed eucalyptus. I remember a summer's day, way back when, swimming in someone's pool as ash fell like snowflakes onto our shoulders. I drive by the sprawling shopping centre where I spent Thursday nights, chasing girls. Rows and rows of identical houses flash by. Somewhere in there, in the maze of roundabouts and cul-de-sacs, I could find the bedrooms and backyards where I had all my firsts. If only I had the time. The last song fades out and I change the CD at a red light. I keep going. Driving past used car lots, mechanics, shut up shop fronts, and finally just quiet stretches of farmland. The barren earth is familiar, desolate and comforting.

This is what we did, me and the boys in a Holden on the highway—sizzling asphalt, beers between our knees, hip hop blaring, greasy hash browns in our hands and the burn of a seatbelt on bare skin.

Eventually we'd stop somewhere, in a park or parking lot, talk and talk as night fell around us. Our phones buzzed aggressively signaling curfews forgotten in laughter and smoke.

Now, I hold a Marlboro against the steering wheel and blow the smoke into the blurring landscape that I know like the back of my hand. I think of Marko, back in the day, teaching me how to inhale and how to roll a roach from the red and white cigarette pack. I hold my breath.

We stayed up late, our backs against the barbed wire fence of a local high school, just south of here. We sat in a line facing the basketball court with ripped nets and graffiti. We passed a bong around, waiting for our turn with chins tucked into zipped-up hoodies. Up ahead we could see the trains as they passed through Warwick Farm station. We could hear them rattling for a good while after they disappeared. Sometimes we'd hear a siren in the distance, or the buzzing of a flickering streetlight, but the silence was loudest.

One night a police siren wailed nearby and we were bathed in flashing blue and red lights. I flinched and put the bong behind my back. Marko grabbed my shoulder and yelled, 'Watch out, sick cunt! The pigs are coming!' I shrugged his hand off quickly and caught him with a left hook. 'Bro, put a little spin in that wrist. You might as well be tickling me,' he winked. Then he packed me another cone and said, 'Relax, cuz. If they were coming for us, I bet there'd be more of 'em.' We all laughed because it was easy to laugh back then. We were untouchable. We were sixteen.

In my last summer in Sydney, I spent long humid days on the outskirts of the western suburbs, in a farm rented in someone else's name. Roosters called at dawn, tractors and lawnmowers started, cars and trucks thundered down the highway. I was always up first. I put the kettle on, emptied the overflowing ashtrays, picked up crushed tinnies and empty bottles, patted the dogs while they slept and watched the sky getting brighter. Every morning Marko put on a hi-vis shirt and waved to the neighbours across the fence. In the paddock between the houses there were two black horses, sturdy looking with glistening manes. Something about their slow, deliberate paces was calming. Every morning Marko and I watched them as we drank milky instant coffee on the porch, smoked a few ciggies then jumped into his car and blasted Biggie through the speakers.

In the daytime, I followed him through sparsely furnished flats in rundown high-rises, with a soundtrack of chatter that was sometimes English, sometimes Serbian, depending on the details. 'What's with the hi-vis?' I asked him once, sitting on a lumpy couch half-watching a talk show, turning a knife over in my hand. 'So the neighbours think I'm going to work,' he answered, with a tilt of the head and a tap on the nose, while he chopped weed into an empty cereal bowl. A black flag with a skull and crossbones loomed above our heads proclaiming *freedom or death* with the elaborate detailing of the Cyrillic alphabet. Skinny teenagers with tight fades darted through the apartment with speed coursing through their blood, running errands for him and speaking only in English.

We would return to the farm after sundown. If the driveway was littered with cars, I sat on the porch, watching for high beams on the road. Men paced about the yard, their faces obscured by shadows. They passed around a warm plate with neat white lines, snorting loudly and rubbing an index finger along their gums, before shuffling into the night. I waited on the porch while they worked, gazing at the sky as it lit up with stars, feeling the pulse of a secret world.

If no one else was around, Marko reluctantly asked for my help. 'Just five more minutes,' I would say, hesitating. I would inevitably oblige, packing soil into pots, stooping in a humid jungle protected from the outside by tarps and heavy padlocks, watering and picking, speaking in hushed tones below heat lamps. I learned how to navigate the shadows of night, feeling with tentative hands in the darkness, treading carefully. I thought of the lambs in the next paddock and the songs we sang as children. Touching the plants, I thought about allergic reactions. When we sparred, Marko used to lean right into my face and say, 'You have to stop being afraid of getting hit. Or you'll never move forward.' I listened carefully for sirens. I was always sure they were coming.

I arrive with a sharp turn off the highway, locking the car and making my way across the vast parking lot towards the entry. Beads of sweat run down my back and I have to squint to see where I am walking, but still a shiver spins and courses through my body. Inside, I am confronted with grimy walls, chaotically decorated with Corrective Services posters, a long line of people, the stench of cigarettes and urine. I shuffle towards the glass panel slowly, in time with everyone else. Behind the glass a large guard punches computer keys with one finger and leans back in his chair, as if he has all the time in the world. The line of waiting people grows and grows.

The man at the front of the line has a tattoo on his neck, a name in slanting cursive letters. He is wearing shorts and a backwards cap, shuffling from foot to foot as he slides his ID to the guard behind the glass. 'Jason doesn't have visiting privileges this week,' the guard says, sliding the ID back and stretching his arms slowly above his head. There's a back and forth for a minute. The man smacks the glass with an open palm, snarls 'You dirty cunt,' and walks out of the room with arms swinging. A guard follows after him and everyone in the line cranes their neck to see what happens next. I tuck my hands into my pockets and keep my eyes on my beat-up Nikes, shuffling along on the checkered tiles.

When my turn arrives, I slide my ID through the slit in the glass and sign the form. My fingerprints and retinas are scanned. I put my phone and wallet in a locker. Then I am buzzed through to a room where I take my shoes and belt off. A guard with a creased forehead and thick hairy arms chews gum, metal detector in hand. He says, 'You got gum? Spit it out!' Above his head a sign reads: No gum, no jewellery, no gifts, no headwear, no scarves. I put my shoes and belt back on, nod at the guard. As the doors slam shut behind me, a heavy clang of metal, I feel my heartbeat speed up. I take a deep breath and walk forward.

In the next room, the people from the waiting line embrace men in white jumpsuits with *visits* printed on the back. Everyone sits on low stools around stainless steel tables. The far wall is lined with bins, overflowing with the bright wrappers of vending machine snacks. A row of guards lines the doorway, staring straight ahead. I sit on one of the stools, the steel cold on the back of my thighs. One of the guards snaps, 'You can't sit there! That's where the inmate sits.' I mumble an apology as I shift to another spot.

Everything here makes me feel like I'm back on the farm, seeing this happen before it happened. This is what I feared in the night, when I sat on the porch watching the road, my gut twisting. I hold my breath and wait for Marko.

As I wait I think of drives with the boys—Dr Dre through the subwoofers, servo doughnuts and late night kebabs, texting girls and smoking Marlboro Reds. Or the quiet nights when we sat hunched over the harvested plants, picking the fat buds off them and burying the empty branches out in the paddocks. We became men with hard faces, men with secrets.

I left with two boxes of books and a handful of photos. If I thought of the boys, it was of the creased polyester of school uniforms, arm wrestling, bad jokes, bongs made of Gatorade bottles. In this desolate place, I look down at my Nikes and remember how we used to talk about living in the mountains someday, somewhere with fresh air. I sit and wait. And I think of all the lives I might have lived if I had stayed.

Coffee and Copper

Sophie MacNeill

On her first morning back, Samira leaves the house early. Breakfast is simple: two thick slices of soft white bread sandwiching cheese and cured meat, devoured hastily over the kitchen sink. The first meal she's eaten in her home country since she was seven years old. Samira wonders vaguely if she should have insisted on something more ceremonious—perhaps taken her aunt out for breakfast in a cafe—but she'd woken well before sunrise, feeling disjointed.

After Heathrow, she'd taken a flight to Budapest and then a coach, arriving in Sarajevo late the night before. Her aunt had picked her up from the bus terminal in a tiny red hatchback that had juddered violently as they sped out of the carpark. Samira had been surprised by her aunt's appearance; she was no longer the stern, hard-faced spectre of her childhood. The older woman's brooding, angular, features were now softened by a layer of creased fat, and the sweet, musky smell of her perfume hung in the heated interior of the car. It reminded Samira of her mother, who wore the same scent. She relaxed immediately, although the car continued to shake as they made their way back to the house.

Her aunt placed one hand on Samira's as she drove. 'I know you won't really remember me Mira, but I have thought about you often. And I am so sorry for your loss. For all of your losses.'

Samira had looked out the car window at the darkened silhouettes of her new-old city. 'As am I, for yours, tetka.'

Now, after only a few hours of fitful sleep, Samira can think only of coffee. As a child she'd never spent much time in the cafes of Sarajevo, but they are the key setting in many of her parent's old photographs. It seems they'd wiled away their youth in those Ottoman-style coffee shops, sipping the traditional thick brew from copper cups, inhaling fruit-flavoured shisha smoke, and talking animatedly with their bohemian-looking friends. Samira has spent hours looking over those old sepia photos, trying to get a sense of who her parents had been. Their long hair and wide grins were evidence of a life before, something greater, more full of possibility than the one they have in New York—worn-down, grey, a life defined by hard physical labour and carefully counted coin—a librarian and a graduate student reduced to cleaners, saving every spare cent they had so they could send their daughter to university.

Their life was built on the first one, cultivated in the many cafes that lined the streets of Sarajevo's old town, a life of long philosophical discussions and wasted afternoons. Samira is sure she was borne from that kind of life. If she can sit in one of those cafes, hold warm copper to her lips and inhale the rich bittersweet scent of bosanka kafa, she might be able to get some of it back, erasing some of the pain from the last few years. Hana, Tom ... How many times would she have to start over?

Walking down the steep hill from her aunt's place towards Sarajevo's old town, Baščaršija, she keeps her gaze averted from the large cemetery that lines one side of the street. Most of the tombstones are white and new-looking, with fresh roses on the graves. Sarajevo has become a city marked by these graveyards. They blanket the hillsides—a constant reminder of what has been lost. The green-tinged sky threatens snow, and the ground is frozen, covered in a layer of frost that sparkles in the early morning sun. Samira turns away and hurries to the bottom of the hill.

A small cube of brown sugar rests between Samira's front teeth. She brings the copper cup to her lips, attempting to sip coffee through the packed granules like her father showed her. Despite a small amount of liquid dribbling onto her chin, she's mostly successful, sweetness dissolving into the thick gritty liquid as it hits her tongue. She giggles. The old woman who served her looks over from her small table by the shop entrance, grinning. Samira looks away, a hot pressure building in her chest. It feels like her heart is expanding, pushing against her sternum. For a moment, she imagines herself split open. Connected to something beyond herself, beyond grief. Seated inside a tiny cafe in a narrow alleyway of Baščaršija, she perches on a low stool, drinking the longed-for bosanka kafa like a real Sarajevan. Through the open shop window, Samira watches as early risers, tourists and locals make their way across the cobblestones. The locals move briskly but the tourists meander, stopping occasionally to look in a shop window or snap a photo. Leaning back against the rough, stone wall behind her, Samira closes her eyes. All her desires are satiated, for now.

A high-pitched wailing startles her and she spills coffee onto her hand. A ginger cat streaks down the alley, followed by a pack of stray dogs. The animals' uncut nails click violently against the cobblestones. The cat bolts down an adjacent alley, the dogs following closely behind. Their collective clattering and wailing fades in the distance. The woman at the café entrance curses under her breath, before returning to her newspaper. Samira sucks the spilt coffee off her hand—bitterness and salt mingle in her mouth. She picks up her own copy of the Bosnian-language paper, resting next to the copper coffee tray.

The front page has a large, full-colour photo of refugees in a camp near the sea. Syrian, she presumes, studying the women's colourful hijab and long robes. Samira can't read the words, but assumes the camp is somewhere on the coast in Croatia. Or maybe Greece. She opens the paper and is confronted with more images, a two-page spread. In one, a woman squats in the sand, a baby strapped to her chest in a shabby looking grey wrap. Samira wonders if it had once been white. It looks like cotton, now stiff with dust and salt. She can feel the weight of a babe against her chest and the fabric wrap brushing against the fine hairs on her neck. Studying the photo more closely, she brings the page up to her eye line. The woman peers into the camera, into Samira's eyes. Two older children—both girls—sit in front of the woman. They look towards the camera but not at it, entranced by something in the distance. Samira closes the paper and puts it back on the table. She swallows the last few drops of now-cold coffee. Walking over to the old woman to pay, Samira's cheeks grow hot as she fumbles over the unfamiliar currency. Blushing, she heads in the direction of the cat.

Exiting the narrow alley, Samira cuts across the main square of Baščaršija. The area is overrun with pigeons. Small groups of them take flight as people walk through the open space. Their speckled grey wings beat against the darkening sky, green necks flashing metallic. Fanning out, they hang suspended for a moment in the air, before settling back around the base of the famous Sebilj fountain. The surrounding scene feels familiar to Samira, but her thoughts slide over any attempt to place a memory there. She remembers an old wives' tale from her childhood: anyone who drinks water from the Sebilj's tap will return to Sarajevo. She can't remember who'd told her the tale, and she doesn't recall ever drinking the water herself. They'd left so abruptly there hadn't even been time to pack a bag, let alone indulge in superstition. The square was already pockmarked by sniper fire, ever-present during the siege of the city.

From the other side of the square comes the sound of repetitious, tinny beats. Samira follows, entering Coppersmith Alley, the curved street that has housed copper craftsmen for hundreds of years. The alley is lined with small shops and display tables, mostly coffee pots and cups, but also plates, jewel-studded trinket boxes, vases, jewellery, and other items. Some are a dark, burnished bronze, others gleaming copper or silver. Rows of shining plates hang suspended from shop awnings, with classic Bosnian scenes beaten into them: the arched Ottoman bridge at Mostar; famous mosques; the Medjugorje apparition of the Virgin Mary. Samira picks up one of the classic hourglass-shaped coffee pots, disturbed to see 'Made in China' stamped into the bottom. Moving further along the alley, she searches for a store that still carries only hand-beaten pieces. A tray of rings with intricate designs catches her eye. A middle-aged man emerges from the shop and sits on a stool by the front door. He has thick white brows, deep-set eyes, and a large, protruding belly. Samira can't help but be reminded of her dad. The man smiles up at her, as if reading her thoughts.

'*Dobro jutro.*' He nods at Samira, then gestures at the jewellery display. '*Molim vas, probajte ih.*'

She shakes her head. 'I'm very sorry, I don't speak Bosnian.'

He lifts one impressive eyebrow. 'Oh, American! I could have sworn you were a Sarajevan. You have the look. Where are you from?'

'Well, I am from here originally, but we left just after the war started. I grew up in New York.'

'Ah, a returnee. This is very good.' He stands abruptly and walks back inside the shop. A few moments later he returns, right fist closed over something. He takes Samira's hand and places the object in her palm. She looks down at a small, delicate ring made from dull, matte copper. The design is simple; a perfect circle in the centre surrounded by four tight swirls of beaten metal. 'This one is antique. Made by my father.'

'It's beautiful.' Samira fumbles with her purse. 'I'll take it. How much?'

'No, no. It is for you. Please. A welcome home gift.' He smiles widely. 'Now get home with you, young lady. It's about to snow!'

Samira looks to the sky. The cloud cover has thickened, casting a muted grey light over the world and obscuring the mountains that surround the city. The exposed skin on her face prickles. The air feels like it's tightening around her. Light snow begins to fall, as if the man's words have released something. She turns back to say goodbye to him, but he's already retreated inside. She slips the ring into her pocket and walks on. Looking at the sky, with the ring in her palm, she has that feeling again, briefly, of being split open—her heart radiating outwards, reaching beyond itself.

She pulls the hood of her coat up over her hair. The tips of her ears sting. Turning towards the main square, she notices a small group of young girls walking down the alley towards her. They wear long skirts, brightly coloured but ragged. Their dark hair hangs long and loose. Roma children, Samira thinks. She's read that they are often found begging for money in the streets of Sarajevo. She fumbles with her purse again, wanting to get some change ready. Her hands are clumsy with cold. But the girls don't stop or even look at Samira as they walk past. They begin to sing in high voices. Arms linked, they sway in unison as they continue down the alley.

Samira turns to watch them. Their sweet voices are high and childish, catching at the edges of the copper-beating din coming from some of the shops. The girls at the front of the group are taller, and seem older. Around thirteen, she'd guess. A few younger ones trail behind, holding hands. The smallest, a girl barely older than a toddler, stops just in front of Samira and looks back over her shoulder. She's fairer than the others, her hair a light chestnut. Her pale skin is freckled across the nose. Samira gasps. Her daughter, Hana, didn't live past a year, but Samira has spent many long nights imagining what she might have looked like as she grew up. This girl is the embodiment of all her imaginings. They stare at each other. Samira's breath quickens; she feels unable to push the thinning air down past her chest. The snow falls faster, heavier, creating a gauzy curtain between Samira and her surroundings. Pressure builds in her ears, but she can still make out the muffled copper beats, and the sweet, high-pitched song of the Roma girls trailing off into the distance. The little girl giggles and breaks eye contact. She turns and runs after her group. Samira follows, trailing the girl's swirling red skirt, just visible through the snowfall.

Samira struggles to keep pace, twisting and turning down Baščaršija's maze-like alleys, shoes slapping against cobblestone. A girl runs ahead of her, laughing, and sometimes stopping, as if she wants to be followed. Copper beats. Tang of coffee brewing in the air. Salt on her tongue. Sharp snowflakes kissing bare cheeks. The alley maze blossoms into a familiar map of names and landmarks as she follows the girl with freckles on her nose and flowing chestnut hair. It feels like a memory, like running through her childhood. Through the streets of a Sarajevo long gone. Or perhaps just forgotten.

The flash of red skirt disappears into the distance. She can no longer hear any singing or laughing. The beating of copper remains a faint monotonous noise in the background. She has re-emerged into the open market square but can't see anything through the heavy snow. Walking a few paces forward, she almost trips on the steps of the Sebilj fountain. How did she end up back here? Her aunt's neighbourhood is still a twenty-minute walk up a nearby hill. She climbs the few steps to the base of the Sebilj and huddles beneath the fountain's narrow roof. Several pigeons have taken cover in the basin below the fountain tap. They press against each other for warmth, feathers puffed and necks pulled in. Samira shivers, pushing her hands deep into her pockets. She feels the ring in her right pocket and clasps it tight in her palm. I'll wait here until the snow lets up a little, she thinks, then I'll make my way back up the hill.

She pictures all those white graves buried in snow.

Standing on the threshold of her aunt's house, Samira is frozen in the open doorway. The heavy front door key drops from her hand and clatters against the floorboards. She holds her left foot aloft, mid-slide out of the boot. Gripping the heavy wooden doorframe with her right hand, Samira attempts to regulate her breathing. Her throat feels tight, swollen.

'Is that you, Mira?' Her aunt calls from the kitchen at the back of the apartment.

The older woman peers into the long hallway. She inspects Samira from a distance, wiping her hands on a tea towel she has tucked into her waistband. As she shuffles down the hall in her house slippers, the smell of hot baked cinnamon follows her from the kitchen.

'You're letting snow in.' She pulls Samira inside, gently, and shuts the door behind her.

Samira stares down at the top of her aunt's head, entranced by the haphazard layers of wiry greys bristling with static from the chill.

'How was your walk?' Stooping to pull off Samira's left boot, she lines up the pair on a cluttered shoe rack by the door. She places a pair of worn slippers by Samira's feet—a passive reminder of the correct etiquette. Straightening her back, she turns to face her niece. Her wide-set, reddish-brown eyes match Samira's perfectly. How could her child-self have been scared of this warm, gentle woman? Samira slumps against the wall. Her aunt raises one drawn-on eyebrow and steps towards her.

'What happened? Are you alright?'

Samira crosses her arms, her upper body shivering. 'I ... I saw her ... but it couldn't have been Hana.' She frowns, looking at the floor. A small pool of melted snow is slowly trickling towards her socked feet.

'Your sister?'

'Sister?' Samira lifts her face, staring again into her aunt's kohl-rimmed eyes. She wonders if everything her aunt had lived through during the war might've caused some early dementia. Or maybe this kind of mental confusion is genetic, she thinks, cringing at what just happened on her walk, at the way she'd chased her daughter's doppelgänger through the streets, as if Hana had even lived to be a girl that age. 'I meant my daughter. I know that's crazy. Impossible.'

'Oh. Your baby.' Her aunt sighs. 'I never got to meet her. So they were both Hana ... Did you name her after your sister?'

The long hallway stretches itself out before Samira's eyes. A vision of the girl with the chestnut hair runs through her mind, down the hallway, past the graveyard, through the alleyways of Baščaršija, into the market square congested with pigeons. Samira is following her, but stops herself from stepping into the open square. Snow is falling. The girl is still running. It feels like a memory. The clatter of nails on cobblestones. Pigeons are taking flight. Someone is wailing. A red skirt twirls. The clattering stops. Samira grips the stone wall with her right hand, looking at the Sebilj fountain.

Paper Cranes

Ruth Armstrong

Alice's husband, Paul, loves overnight flights. As they board the 9.30pm to Tokyo he tells her yet again what a boon it is to save on the first and last night's accommodation while making the most of their precious days off. Although Alice does her best to look agreeable, privately she is unconvinced. They have done this many times before, and the night of lost sleep always ensures that she starts her holiday feeling alienated and exhausted. But she understands that Paul's motivation has little to do with efficiency; he simply cannot contemplate the idea of sitting inactive on a plane for hours, then arriving at their destination in time for bed. He is a restless man, which has its pros and cons.

In the darkened cabin of the plane, Alice curls into the window moulding and Paul kicks off his shoes and sprawls backwards, flicking through the inflight entertainment. They are well-practised in these long stretches of peripatetic solitude. A decade ago, when they first met, they kept their relationship secret by heading out of Sydney every weekend. Their marriage owes a lot to the low-lit cabins of cars and planes, but there will be no stories or strategising tonight. Tonight it feels like they are just two people who happen to be heading in the same direction.

As the hours pass Alice manages to sleep in snatches. In one fleeting dream she is composing the perfect tweet to link to her research paper. Next time she dozes she's standing at a podium trying to deliver a presentation written in some unknown Arabic script. Phrases from conversations with colleagues and patients circle round in her mind. Then she is in an unfamiliar kitchen, carefully preparing a batch of tempura made with thin fillets of fish. She holds up one of the translucent strips and finds it has a tiny, worried face. She smiles at it reassuringly before dipping it in batter and placing it in the hot oil.

Alice awakes with a surge of nausea and wonders again why they have persisted with this holiday. They have had it booked for months, ever since returning from a work trip that left them intrigued by the old Japanese capital of Kyoto. With the turmoil of the past few weeks she has come close to cancelling, but Paul is adamant it will do them both good to get away, maybe even try some cycling in the countryside: do some of the things they missed on their previous visit.

They arrive to a city that is barely awake and take an express train towards central Tokyo. Alice slumps against the window and stares dazedly out at the countryside; villages of traditional-looking wooden houses and every scrap of spare land devoted to growing rice, then a sudden transition to crowded streets of mid-rise residential buildings, giving way to towering blocks of offices, shops and apartments. When they change at Shinagawa, the station is packed with morning commuters. Alice buys a takeaway coffee that is made over what looks like a Bunsen burner, by two serious women wearing white lab coats and surgical masks.

'Back on the juice,' says Paul. 'Is it any good?'

'It's awful,' she says, offering him a taste. 'I'd forgotten how bad.'

It's late morning when they drag their bags across the marble floor to the reception desk of their Kyoto hotel. The concierge greets them; she's wearing a 1950s hostess-style uniform, in keeping with the building's faded oriental glamour. While Paul checks in, Alice wanders across the foyer to look at a black-and-white photographic exhibition of Japanese waterbirds. On a small platform in one corner she notices a life-sized cardboard tableau of a radiant young bridal couple. When she rejoins Paul he has already booked two bicycles for the duration of their stay and a restaurant for this evening. He consults the notes on his mobile phone.

'There's a place out of town: *Arashyama*?'

'The bamboo grove. Very beautiful and very romantic,' says the concierge.

'And a temple up in the hills nearby?' He shows her an image on the screen.

'*Adashino Nembutsu-ji*, a peaceful place. It also has bamboo but is not so crowded.' She pulls out a printed map, making precise circles around the important landmarks on the cycling route.

'That's tomorrow sorted,' Paul tells Alice.

Up in the room they stand together, looking from the picture window down to the river and the forested mountains beyond. The town is contained in a small basin with tree-lined roads spreading like tendrils into the foothills. Housekeeping has left a light blue origami crane on each of the twin beds and a much smaller one in aqua and silver on the bedside table. Paul holds the tiny crane up to the light and traces a finger over the intricate fold where its body meets its wing.

'I'll go down and ask about a double,' he says, pulling a clean t-shirt from his bag.

'No, leave it,' she tells him too quickly. 'I don't want to end up in a smoking room.'

He looks deflated. 'Okay, well let's change and go out on the bikes.'

'You go. I might stay here. It's raining a bit, and I'm tired.'

She showers and unpacks, then sits on the bed studying the city map, having decided to do her one errand in Kyoto while Paul is otherwise occupied. His niece, who is studying Japanese at school, has asked her to bring home some authentic paper for her origami class. She dresses, pops the smallest crane in her pocket to use as a prop in case of communication problems, and heads out.

Wandering into a series of arcaded streets near the hotel, she realises she is in the right place for paper goods. There are antique bookshops, stalls selling rubber stamps and inks, galleries displaying watercolours and linoleum prints, and several large stationers. The arcades are crowded with women wearing waterproof boots, hurrying around with their colourful raincoats flapping behind them. In the best-looking stationer she buys squares of hand-painted origami paper in several patterns.

Back in the room the two larger origami cranes sit silhouetted on the windowsill, turned as if looking out at the view. She snaps an image on her phone and is amazed, as always, at the technology that allows both the cranes and valley outside to be in focus. On an impulse she shares the image via Twitter, links to her recent publication and tags a few of her colleagues who will understand the reference. 'Cranes in Kyoto: papers from #paedcon15 now online.'

Alice would not usually tweet a holiday snap but, for those in the know, there is a tangible link between the origami cranes and her work. Five months ago she and Paul gave a joint presentation in the grand ballroom of this hotel to an international paediatrics conference. Looking for something to humanise their request for collaborators in a database of rare birth defects, Alice hit upon the hotel's signature origami crane as a symbol of the longevity that parents everywhere desire for their children, initiating what became a unifying motif for the rest of the conference.

The success of the presentation was made more remarkable by the fact that Alice was incapacitated on the day by symptoms of a stomach virus. Still tired and unwell on her return home she discovered that, quite unintentionally and at forty-three, she was pregnant.

They arrive for dinner early and are shown to a table on a temporary bamboo balcony, overhanging the river. For the first half hour they have the company of a group of young businessmen, shouting to each other across the tables and alternating sake with beer until they look dishevelled and world-weary. After a formal presentation to the only older man in the group, they all slouch out, briefcases in-hand and jackets slung over their shoulders. When her food finally arrives, Alice realises she is almost too tired to eat and even Paul's appetite seems to have waned. He eats a little then pushes his plate aside and reaches for Alice's hand.

'I was wondering, today, have you told your mother about what happened?'

'No, why?'

'Surely she'd want to know.'

Alice shakes her head.

'There's no need,' she says. 'Mum told me at my fortieth, she wasn't expecting grandkids.'

'I told Gareth.'

'You know mum actually said she admired me. Said she wished she'd had the sense not to have kids.'

They both laugh. Alice's mother gives them plenty of material.

They are silent as the waiter removes their plates.

'I wish you hadn't told Gareth,' says Alice.

Paul stands to follow the waiter out to the register.

'I had to tell someone.'

The following morning, they follow the river westwards before turning sharply back into the busy streets. The pavements are smooth and wide enough to ride on, and she keeps up with Paul fairly easily so that they make it to their first stop for the day, *Kinkaku-ji,* right at opening time. Despite this, the area is already crowded with bus-loads of teenagers, ready to join the queue for a glimpse of the gold-clad temple. They stow the bikes and head towards the entry but are quickly accosted by a group of about eight high schoolers, neatly dressed in black and white uniforms. A man in his twenties, also in uniform, speaks for the group.

'Good morning. We are from the *Tanagawa* Middle School in Tokyo. My students are learning English and would like to have a short conversation with you.'

A girl and a boy step forward shyly, each holding a booklet, which Alice can see contains questions written in English.

'What country are you from?' says the girl.

'What places will you visit in Kyoto?' The questions go on. 'What work do you do in Australia?'

'I am a doctor for children and my husband is a statistician—a person who works with numbers.'

The teacher interrupts. 'Just one more question.'

The boy steps forward and peers into his booklet. 'Do you have any children?'

When the group moves on, Paul takes Alice's arm.

'Let's ride out to *Arashyama* first and come back here this afternoon. This crowd is doing my head in.'

It's a single lane, sealed road to *Arashyama,* which starts off winding through suburbia, and descends slowly into a farming valley. For the first few kilometres Alice feels monstered by the buses and trucks but as the road becomes less busy she starts to enjoy the rural surroundings. There's a light mist of rain, and the air smells like damp earth and cows. They stop at a noodle bar for cold *soba* and iced tea, and find the right road to take them up the hill to the temple Paul wants to see.

Finally, they reach an unassuming stone gate with a wooden sign indicating where to leave the bikes. The track down to the temple is a series of widely-spaced, earth and stone stairs, passing through a bamboo grove, and this entry alone makes Alice glad they have come. The long thin trunks reach out above them almost into a guard of honour as they pass through, the sparse foliage at the top filtering the light.

She follows Paul into a large clearing crowded with thousands of small, identical monuments of stacked stones that look like little, grey snowmen. Around the outside are mature cyprus and oak trees, and the ground is covered in vibrant green moss. There are a few people gathered outside a bunker-like building in the centre of the monuments, and Alice and Paul gravitate towards the English-speaking voice of a sinewy Japanese woman in her forties, who is conducting a tour.

'This is *Adashino Nembutsu-ji*,' she says. 'Many centuries ago, people from the villages near here brought the bodies of their loved ones to this hill after death. Some were so poor that they could not afford a burial or a tombstone. The bodies were left exposed to the elements with nothing to mark their resting place. These stone monuments—more than eight thousand in all—are simple buddhas. We use them to honour the souls of all those who have died without a memorial.'

The guide pauses as several people wander away. Alice is surprised to see Paul move closer to ask the woman a question.

'Is it true that you also hold *Mizuko* memorial services here?' he asks.

The guide nods, 'Yes, *Mizuko kuyo* is held at many temples in Japan. This is a ceremony to pray for babies that have died before birth. Here the ceremony is held once every month'.

She turns to reconvene her group and Alice and Paul are alone. Paul takes off his sunglasses and she can see that his eyes are red-rimmed.

'Doesn't this place make you feel anything?' he asks.

'It's very beautiful and moving,' she says, 'but we're not Buddhist. There's nothing here for us. I don't even know why we came.'

He takes a few steps towards the main building, before turning back to her.

'Okay, fine, let's go.'

Paul sets off. He cycles down the narrow streets, past the tiny shops Alice had hoped to explore on their way down, weaving around parked cars and minibuses. As far as she can tell he's not using his brakes at all. She sees an elderly street vendor whose eye she had caught on the way up, selling intricate prints depicting the stone mounds from the temple. As Paul disappears around a corner she stops to buy one, then resumes her ride at an easier pace. A bit further down a police car with its lights flashing blocks a side road, looking incongruously modern in this idyllic setting. After riding downhill for a long time she notices that the landmarks are unfamiliar. The buildings have thinned out too quickly; the road is now an uneven track with a wide verge; she passes a rice field and a derelict house that she doesn't remember, then reaches a T intersection of two roads that look like farm tracks and realises she is lost.

Straight ahead the path tapers of into another section of bamboo forest before closing in altogether. Alice wheels her bike carefully into the bamboo, and stands looking up at the long stems at close range. She hears the trunks creaking gently, and the background sound of the leaves like light rain, and wonders what it must have been like to struggle through this thick vegetation carrying the body of a loved one. The way up the hill must have been agonising, she thinks, but she finds herself also wondering about way back down to the world of the living in the valley. In her work, she has seen immense fortitude in the face of death, but rarely what comes after for the survivors.

Her mobile rings.

'Did you see the police car? You were supposed to go that way.' Paul always starts his calls as if in mid-conversation.

Alice disconnects without replying, returns to the road and starts the slow ride uphill.

She finds him sitting beside his bike on a low bank in front of a quaint wooden building. There's a sign above him in Japanese characters that might say 'welcome' or 'keep off' or something else altogether. How would Alice know? She stops in front of him, still straddling her bike.

'You know I'm hopeless with directions. Why didn't you wait?'

Paul stays where he is; beneath his sunglasses his cheeks are mottled and puffy, and she notices his knees are stained with grass and mud.

'What's happening to us?' he says.

Standing over him, the anger drains out of her.

'I stuffed up. That's what's happened. I made the call to have all the testing done. I knew it wasn't completely safe but I wanted to be certain everything was normal.'

He looks puzzled. 'It was hardly reckless; less than a one percent chance of pregnancy loss, the obstetrician told me afterwards. Said she'd never had it happen before. Do you really think I blame you?'

Alice sits on the bank beside him.

'What did Gareth say when you told him?' she asks.

'He cried.'

'Gareth cried for our baby?'

'Yep.'

'He's a good friend.'

They sit in silence for a few minutes, cooled by a slight breeze coming up the valley. Finally, Paul stands and offers her his hand, 'Up there, at the temple,' he says, 'I just wanted to acknowledge it together somehow. If we can't even do that, how can we move on?'

She remains hunched on the bank, arms by her sides. 'Maybe we can't,' she says quietly.

Paul fusses around readying himself for the ride home but still Alice doesn't move.

'I'll head off,' he says. 'I'll be down the road, near the river.'

When she can no longer see him she gathers up her things. Feeling in the pocket of her rain jacket for a tissue, her hand finds the tiny origami crane, now damp and crushed, its colours smudged. She pulls it out and studies it for a while, examining the perfect folds where its body meets its wings.

She puts it carefully back in her pocket, then hops on her bike and rides as fast as she dares, down the hill to where she hopes her husband will be waiting.

Countdown to New Year

Kerrie Knox

For the last ten months I've imagined meeting you. I've directed scenes in my head, clapperboard on hand, ready to call 'cut' if it's not ideal. I've almost perfected it now. I'd stroll up those fractured concrete steps that weave to your door, stand on your brown coir mat, and press the faded beige doorbell. Your white timber door would swing open and you'd peer through the brown diamonds of the security door that you keep locked to protect your little family.

And I'd tell you who I was.

I wait outside your house, on nights like tonight, and I play out the same scene over and over.

It's cold tonight. The Melbourne winter is leeching into my ten-year-old Corolla. This car was my first big purchase, a sign I was now an adult. I'd been patient, saving every spare cent until I could ditch the P-plates and trade my bomb for something nice. Surely two years of safe driving was enough to make me immune to dings and dents. Such is the reasoning of a twenty year-old.

I haven't changed out of my work clothes because I haven't been home from work yet. I dashed from the office to the shops and now my charcoal skirt is scrunched up around my thighs and the matching jacket is creased from pressing against the steering wheel. I crane forward for a line of sight to your porch, waiting for the moment you flip the switch and plunge your doorstep into darkness. You're turning the light off much later now.

The shopping centre was busy tonight, filled with noisy toddlers and fractious teens. Even the in-centre audio seemed louder than usual. It's taking longer to shop for you now. I agonised this evening over getting you the grapefruit hand cream or the linen tea-towel, dotted with coffee cups. I try to buy gifts you wouldn't buy yourself. I stare at lacy scarves, breathe in the scent of French perfume and I imagine your fingers brushing over them with desire. You wouldn't buy them though, would you? There'd always be something more important: new shoes for little feet, the dreaded electricity bill, or a crisp white invoice from Le Pine Funerals.

Darren hated shopping with me. 'Get in, get what you need and get out,' he used to say. He would never have lost hours searching for the perfect gift.

It's been nine weeks since I've seen Darren. I promised him I'd visit again soon but even to me it sounded like a line. I leave it a little longer between each visit, holding out until I can no longer tolerate the nudge of my conscience. I'm getting stronger.

I did love him. The absence of us is like the molar I had extracted last year. My tongue keeps searching the spot, half expecting it to have grown back.

I anticipated a scene on that first visit to the prison. I expected Darren to fire recriminations at me, like missiles, lay blame at my feet as he'd done so often in the past. I'd even pictured some burly, gruff-faced officer dragging him away and Darren shouting, 'This wouldn't have happened if you'd been with me that night'.

I'd scream: 'This wasn't my fault. This wasn't my doing.'

Instead, Darren grasped my hand and squeezed. 'I appreciate you coming,' he said, 'it means a lot to me.'

'You okay?' I asked.

'I miss you,' he said, squeezing my hand again.
Darren.

Were you in court the day they sentenced Darren? I hadn't intended to go. I changed my mind an hour before it was scheduled, rushing from work. I told my boss I was meeting a new client, at their office. He waved me away without raising his head. By the time I left I was so late I had to sprint the last four blocks, through a throng of lunchtime diners, thick across the footpath, a human obstacle-course.

Courtrooms are smaller than I imagined. I'd pictured it like *Law and Order*, cold hard surfaces and open space for lawyers to parade around. Instead, it was like a movie theatre. Cosy and carpeted. Everyone so close.

I sat huddled in the back row watching the bob of Darren's Adam's apple. I could see the faint sheen on his forehead and the rapid rise and fall of his chest. The judge began, lamenting the fact that some people took so long to learn—three prior convictions, licence suspended twice, still the defendant had not been deterred. Darren caught my eye briefly as the sentence was handed down. Eight years.

Darren dropped his chin to his chest. I waited until he was escorted away but he didn't look back.

I was seven years old when my father died. The same age as your eldest child. He left for work one morning and never returned. My mother tried explaining it—scaffolding snapping, a large fall, badly hurt. I'd never known anyone who'd died before. I thought it only happened to old people.

Before he'd left that morning, Dad swept me into his arms like I was a toddler, pressing his lips close to my ear. 'We're finishing up this bloody job today, on time, and I'm getting a bonus. So I'm bringing home a surprise, something nice for your mum and you. Don't tell your mum, though,' he whispered. 'It's our secret.'

I didn't. Ever.

For the next couple of weeks, our home became busier than it had ever been. Cookies and cakes and casseroles arrived, wrapped in tea-towels like presents. My teacher pulled me aside after class the day I returned. She thrust a stuffed pink bear into my arms.

'I'm so sorry, Michelle,' she said. 'If you ever need to talk to someone, you just come and find me.'

Two weeks later she ordered me out of class to pick up rubbish because I'd been daydreaming. The first thing I did when I returned home that day was grab the bear off my bed and race outside to the bin. I tossed it in, pushing it down deep, hiding it under wilted bouquets of flowers.

Darren's sister called me on New Year's morning. She never phoned me, never gave more than a clipped acknowledgement of my existence. The time was six twenty-two; the caller i.d. Claire—Darren's sister. I've got all their numbers: Darren's dad and mum, his two brothers.

'They'll be your family one day,' Darren declared one evening as I punched contacts into a new mobile, 'so you should have their numbers'.

I never called them. Why would I?

Claire's tone was different that morning. Anxiety had shaved off the sharp edges and I buckled under her request.

'Please come to the hospital,' she said. 'There's been an accident. He's asking for you.'

In a haze I threw on the clothes that were dumped on the end of my bed and made the thirty-minute journey to the hospital in twenty. Darren's voice played in my head, an endless loop. I barely registered the radio reports, celebrations around the globe.

Darren and I broke up five times that year. Each time we were apart a little longer and each stint seemed to stretch us further. We became like worn elastic, losing our ability to bounce back. By the end of the year we'd been apart for two months.

'This has to end, Darren. I'm sick of the fighting. I'm sick of this life.' How many times did I say those words?

But there was always a reason to reunite, an invisible tug, drawing me back to him. Soon we'd be screaming at each other again, arguing over whose turn it was to put the bins out—why I'd bought new shoes—why he wouldn't call if he planned on getting so smashed he couldn't get home.

At the funeral, I slipped into the last vacant row, grateful there were enough mourners for me to fade into the background. I shuffled inch-by-inch along the shiny timber pew until I could see you clearly.

You were in the front row, of course. Your children sat beside you, three boys and one girl. Your daughter sat closest, her ponytail barely reaching above the back of the seat. Their heads rose in unison as the black-suited man stepped towards the altar. He bowed his head and walked to the pulpit. He spoke slowly, his voice strong and calm.

He spoke of a loving husband—devoted father, dependable son, loyal friend. A man who drove his taxi after dinner, same as always, earning a living for his family—New Year's Eve too lucrative to refuse. A man who took great care to deliver each passenger home to their loved ones. A man whose misfortune placed him in the middle of an intersection as a speeding, drunk driver ran a red light. I fled the church as the pall-bearers rose to take their places.

Three weeks before New Year I bumped into Darren. I was leaving work and he stepped out of the coffee shop directly opposite my building. He caught my eye, raised his eyebrows, and mouthed, 'Oh'. A car blasted its horn as he stepped into the traffic.

'What a coincidence,' he said after he crossed the street.

He was unshaven and his faded Nirvana t-shirt had a coffee stain on Kurt Cobain's forehead.

'How about dinner?' He suggested.

'I don't think...'

'I miss you, Shel.'

I pushed his hand away, pretending I didn't notice he was still wearing the ring I gave him for his birthday.

'I have to go.'

It's almost eleven and still your porch light burns. There's a sliver of moon tonight and its faint beam shines across the two shopping bags on the passenger seat. I've unpacked and re-packed them twice now, caressing each item, imagining them in your hands. The bags are calico, imprinted with a picture of a great oak, its aged branches canopied to provide shelter.

At the bottom of each of the bags are books. There's a box set of spy stories with a miniature set of binoculars attached to the front. There's a Lego creation book with enough blocks to make seven different vehicles, and three hardcover picture books, all about the adventures of ducks and mice and mischievous puppies.

In the middle of the bags, I've packed treats for you all. There are sweet biscuits shaped like stars and chocolate that melts on your tongue.

At the top of one of the bags is the grapefruit hand cream and the tea towels. Poking out of the other is a furry brown toy puppy with floppy ears and shiny eyes.

I spent New Year's Eve at a girlfriend's house trying to remember what single people did on the last day of the year. It was a few minutes after one a.m. when Darren called. When I saw his name flash up on my phone, I hesitated before I answered. I'd only just shut the door to my flat, hadn't even thrown off the crippling heels I thought a single woman should wear. If the call had come five minutes earlier, I'd have been driving and ignored it. If it had been five minutes later, I would have been in bed.

'Happy New Year.'

Darren's voice was a slur of syllables, words melting into one another.

'I can't live without you,' he said.

'No, Darren.'

'I need you, babe. I'm coming over.'

'You can't drive.'

I knew my protests would be useless. He knew all the back roads. There would be no booze buses in the side streets and less chance of undercover cops pulling him over for clipping the edge of a roundabout, like last time.

I hung up the phone and paced my tiny flat—around the coffee table, into the kitchen, back to the lounge. I pounded the back of the couch, recalling movie nights spent curled around Darren. Not long from now, he'd be sprawled upon it again. Then I made my wish. A circuit-breaker. Darren's Falcon, its front embedded in a tree or an unforgiving light pole. Would that be so bad?

A Shift

Lisa Smithies

I pull the curtain back. The patient is intubated. The ventilator makes its noise: shhh, shhh, shhh. The monitor makes its noise: bip, bip, bip. The night nurse smiles.

'Feels like I haven't seen you for ages. Been away?'

'Three weeks off,' she says.

'Do anything nice?'

'Bali for ten days, then just lying around the house.'

'Heaven.'

'Ready?' She picks up the notes.

'Sure.'

'Twenty-seven year old female, no real history except drugs and alcohol, presented with sudden onset headache two days ago. Busy night. Couldn't be bothered waiting for a scan, so signed herself out. Came back yesterday morning, headache no better. Again couldn't be bothered waiting, so took herself home. Family called an ambulance in the afternoon because she was getting worse. Minor neurology, drowsy and vomiting.'

'Bleed?'

'Big one. Probably extended before ambos got there so she scored a tube and by the time they scanned her she had a big midline shift, small herniation, pupils fixed and dilated. No ICU beds, so she's been in here all night. They're sorting a bed this morning.'

'No theatre?'

'No point.'

I look at the patient. Dyed yellow hair, a few pimples, she could be a teenager. 'Twenty-seven. Shit, that's young.'

'She should have waited.'

'Family here?'

'There's a partner in the Relo's room, not the sharpest tack in the box. Her mum's coming back with the baby.'

We share a look. Baby = Sad.

'I turned the Prope off at 2. ICU are coming to do the assessment and talk to the family about donation. They're not too worried about the obs, just want a MAP above 60 to keep the organs perfused. Numbers haven't changed for hours anyway. Ventilator's on SIMV 400, rate 20, FiO_2 100. They want her a little hyperventilated, even though there's no brain to preserve. PEEP is 5, pressure support 10, she's only little, not even 50 kilos.'

'ICU give a time?'

'They said to call when the mum gets here.'

'Where'd you stay in Bali?'

'We spent half the time at a resort in the mountains and the other half in Kuta. You been?'

'Nah. One day. You wanna go home.'

'Sure. I've restocked most of the room, but you'll need to check the drug and artline boxes.'

'No worries. Go home.'

'Cheers.'

'Sleep well.'

She leaves and it's just me and shhh, shhh, shhh, bip, bip, bip.

I start my assessment.

The head of the bed is at 30 degrees, the way it should be for a patient with raised ICP. I pick up the torch and lift the eyelids. Yeah, they're dilated and, shining the torch across them, fixed.

My mother died of a brain aneurism, not twenty-seven years old but twenty-nine. Her hair was not bottle blonde. It was short, brown and wavy. She would have been lying in a hospital bed like this. She was little too, less than 50 kilos, maybe. You can't tell a person's real weight from old photos. Those polaroids show the shape of her eyes though, smiling crinkles in the corners. But not their colour. Were they blue like mine? Or brown like these eyes, fixed and dilated too.

I put my torch away and move my attention to the mouth. The ET tube is secure. Lip level 23. Size 7, tube clear. I pull back the covers, put my stethoscope to the chest. Good bilateral air entry, heart beat regular, strong. The heart doesn't need the brain, not directly.

I check all my monitor dots are correct. On the right breast is a cheap tattoo—'Shane 4 EVA' inside a pink love heart. I pull the blankets back up over the chest.

I check the artline. Then the CVC. Then the IDC, draining small amounts of urine. Tick.

At the end of the bed, I lift up the blankets and run the back of my pen along the underside of the foot, nothing.

Under the buttocks, I check the sheets are clean and dry. Then I tuck everything back in.

I write all of this down. It's not done if it's not documented.

I imagine my mother's nurse, in another room, another time. She would have been wearing white, rubber-soled shoes with skin coloured stockings. Or, maybe, black leather lace ups with dark stockings, seams straight and true. Starched, stiff and sterile.

A cerebral aneurism occurs when a weakening in the arterial wall causes a bubble, a balloon of sorts that stretches over time, becoming so thin that one day it just pops.

'You okay in here?' Karen pops her head through the curtain and smiles.

'Sure am. You next door?'

'Yep, but I'm empty. Are you working next Saturday?'

'Not sure. Think so.'

'Damn. I fucked up my roster, requested the wrong weekend off. It's my niece's engagement party. Oh well, if I can't find anyone to swap I'll have to chuck a sickie.'

'Good luck.'

'Thanks. Call me if you need anything.'

I turn back. Take in the whole room. Tidy. Bip, bip, shhh.

I always imagined my mother was there one minute, gone the next, but she could have had a headache for days. Did she think she knew better, ignoring her doctor's advice? Or stupidly not going to the doctor at all? No one has told me.

I have this image... she just dropped. There was no warning. I picture her in a blue-flowered dress, yellow sunlight, hanging out the washing, falling onto soft grass. Or, sometimes, she's in the kitchen, her head bouncing off the checkerboard linoleum, red and white.

'Can I come in?' He is scruffy, red-eyed, a wannabe rapper, baseball cap and hanging pants.

I smile. 'I'm Liz, the day nurse. You must be Samantha's partner.'

'Sam. She likes to be called Sam. Yeah... well... ex-partner. We have a baby, but we're not together. At the moment.'

'Come in.' I move a chair to the side of the bed. 'You can sit here.'

He sits and holds her hand.

He starts to cry.

I put a box of tissues on the bed and turn to look at the computer.

He sobs.

I don't turn around.

'Can she hear me?'

'We don't know for sure what the brain is capable of.'

No, she can't hear you.

I paid attention the day we learned about brain bleeds at Uni: a cranium has only a finite amount of space. It's a closed compartment. It has a fixed volume. It contains three components—brain, CSF and blood—the Munroe-Kellie hypothesis states that an increase in any one of these can only be compensated for by a reduction in one of the other two. But brains don't shrink and there's not much CSF to shift, so when those little bastards burst, the blood takes up the space, intracranial pressure builds, pushing the brain down through the base of the cranium into the brainstem, into the spinal column, herniating, cutting off communication. Completely.

'She's really gone, isn't she?'

'Yes.'

'What are you going to do now?'

'A doctor will come and talk to you when Sam's mum gets here.'

'But you can't do anything, that's what the doctor said.'

'That's correct, we can't do anything.'

'She's not here anymore, I can tell.' He touches her face. Then looks up to see if I'm watching. He picks up her hand, kisses it. Then looks up again. He's looking for a nod or a smile. But I don't give it to him.

He wipes the back of his hand across his face with a loud sniff. 'Is there anywhere to get a coffee?'

'The café should be open, in the main foyer.'

'Will they let me back in?'

'Just see the girls at the front.'

'Thanks', he says. And leaves the room.

Shhh, shhh.

The ICU doctor pokes his head in. 'Family here?'

'Partner, not mum.'

'Okay if I quickly do my assessment?'

'No probs.'

I hang the *Do Not Disturb* sign outside the curtain.

'Okay, let's turn the ventilator off,' he says.

Brain death is determined through clinical examination.

He touches a cotton ball to the eye. No blink. He pokes the suction tube down the throat. No gag reflex, no cough. A needle and some ice to the arm. No response.

When you turn off a ventilator, carbon dioxide will build up in the blood. Then the respiratory centre in the brain will kick in.

We both watch the monitor. Bip, bip, bip.

'We've put so much oxygen into her, it'll take a while.'

We watch the monitor. 'Are you permanently in ICU now?'

'Yeah,' he says.

'So you don't love us anymore?'

'I'll always love ED, but ICU is more my style.'

'Tidier. And quieter. And you have doughnuts.'

'Exactly,' he says.

Finally, the CO_2 starts to rise. 42. 43. 44. 45. 'How high do you want it to go?'

'I like to give them til 80.'

When the CO_2 gets high enough, a brain can't resist the drive. When a brain is dead this does not happen. 76. 77. 78. She never starts to breathe. He writes it all down. I take a blood gas. Documentation. Evidence. pH 7.24. $paCO_2$ 85. Still no breathing.

'Alright, we're done.'

I turn the ventilator back on. Shhh. The doctor leaves.

I watch her CO_2 come back down. 82. 81. 80. Bip, bip.

We think of dying as an event, but it's really more a process.

Death is legally determined when an irreversible point in the process has been reached, not when the process has ended. For brain death to be official, it needs to be assessed by two doctors, separately. The patient needs to have normal electrolytes, they need an adequate blood pressure, and they need to be normothermic. They are not dead until they are warm and dead.

I hear a little noise outside the curtain and pop my head out.

'Um. Hello.' Her mother holds a big bouncing baby boy.

I introduce myself and she hugs me tight. She smells like our old next-door neighbour, stale cigarette smoke and incense.

The dad returns too.

I call the doctor back. He introduces himself to the family and takes them into to the Relo's room. They already know the prognosis. This discussion will be about organ donation. Someone so young is a desirable multi-organ candidate. A family needs to sign off.

Karen pops her head back through the curtain, 'Bill brought us a treat. Chocolate or strawberry?' She holds a paper bag in each hand.

'You choose.' She shrugs and hands me one. It's a doughnut with pink icing and sprinkles. 'They having the chat now?' she asks.

'Yep.' I hide the doughnut behind the computer for later.

'Fingers crossed,' she says as she leaves.

They all come back into my room. 'We've decided to go with donation,' the mum tells me. 'That's what she would have wanted.'

'Yeah, it's what she would have wanted,' the dad says.

'We'll care for her in the Intensive Care Unit for a few more hours, while we get everything organised,' the doctor says. 'We'll go up in a few minutes. There'll be some forms for you to sign.'

'Can he give her a kiss?' the dad asks. Beside the bed, he holds the baby like a sack of spuds.

'Of course.' I smile.

He lifts the baby, aeroplane style, towards her face. Hovering above her cheek, the baby babbles and drools. His chubby legs kick. 'Say bye bye to Mummy.'

He steps back. And we give them a moment.

'I think I'd better take him for a walk.'

'Okay.' Sam's mother stays.

'Can I get you anything? A cup of tea?'

She shakes her head, half smiles then goes back to staring blankly at Sam. I move around her, getting the equipment ready for the transfer: portable ventilator, monitor, bag and mask, suction, paperwork. She doesn't move. Is she remembering or imagining? Is there a difference?

All the equipment is ready. The PSA arrives to push the trolley. I touch Sam's mum on the arm, 'It's time to go.' We all squeeze into the lift. No one speaks. Bip, Bip, Bip.

Sam's mum takes a seat in the ICU waiting room. 'I'll let them know you're here. Give them 20 minutes to get her settled and if they haven't come to get you, just press the buzzer.'

Three nurses from neighbouring cubicles come to help transfer Sam over onto her ICU bed. They untangle her lines while I hand over to her primary nurse. 'Twenty-seven year old female, massive intracranial bleed, brain death confirmed by first clinical assessment, donation coordinator has the ball rolling and paperwork started. The mum's in your waiting room. I said you'd call her in 20. Obs are okay, all here as charted.

Once Sam is swapped over to the ICU monitors and ventilators, I turn off my equipment, put it on the trolley and return to the ED in silence. Sam will stay in the ICU until the donation team have everything organised. The family will have time to say goodbye, then she will be taken to theatre. Sam will be given drugs that block sympathetic nervous activity, preventing damage to the retrieved organs, as well as paralysing drugs that prevent her body making any reflex movements, which can be distressing for staff.

Afterword:
Capturing the Unsayable

Julia Prendergast

As I worked with the authors in this collection, I was thinking about what it means to 'handle' someone else's story material. I was contemplating the role of the editor, but more broadly, I was considering how our writing practice is influenced by the work of other writers, as well as those who respond to our writing. It's a fascinating looped interplay—the frayed edges of the writing and reading mind—the temporising spaces.

Drusilla Modjeska suggests that temporising 'can become a form of consciousness' (Modjeska 2002: 76). She writes:

> Temporising [...] is an attitude of mind which develops in certain people who find themselves engulfed, even tipped off balance, by the sadness of the present. *The incurable imperfection in the very presence of the present*, Proust says. As a consequence, they protect themselves with psychological manoeuvres that slip them into other timeframes; in other words they play with time. (Modjeska 2002: 75)

As I became entangled with the stories in this collection, I felt I was in the company of fellow temporisers. In each story, the author examines the sadness and imperfection of the present, through concrete and specific narrative detail, in the realist style. The brevity of short-form fiction makes it an apt vessel for capturing the imperfection of lived experience—the haunting incompleteness of human interaction. Of course, the best short stories are concertina-like, unfolding and contracting as we read them, and thereafter, endlessly.

To engage with work that is in a state of becoming is to bear witness to the writer's attempt to capture the mystery of lived experience—its 'not-enough-ness'. The poet Luke Davies speaks of writing and reading as an act of translating the unsayable. He speaks of the 'spine tingling experience of poetry working in that way [...] it's that moment where it's like I grasp that this poet is approaching translating the unsayable' (Carter, 2016). This is the great joy of reading and the lure of writing—encountering the unsayable through concrete, sensory detail—bearing witness to the creative use of language as an act of deep homage to an otherwise irresolvable idea.

The sadness and imperfection of the present, the irresolvable and the unsayable, puts me in mind of Helen Garner, and of Janet Malcolm, who, by Garner's own admission, has had a profound influence on her writing. In 'The Rapture of Firsthand Encounters' Garner (2016: 181-4) reflects upon Malcolm's incomparable influence, noting that 'Malcolm's way of perceiving the world is deeply dyed by the psychoanalytical view of reality' and drawing attention to Malcolm's claim that 'life is lived on two levels of thought and act: one in our awareness and the other only inferable, from dreams, slips of the tongue, and inexplicable behaviour' (ibid).

The complex juxtaposition of action and intentionality is at the heart of Garner's (2014) book *This House of Grief.* In this text, Garner addresses the complexity of love, familial and romantic, and the context in which an 'ostensibly' loving father, Robert Farquharson, might intentionally drive his car into a river, killing his three boys (Byrne 2016). Garner notes her deep-rooted fascination with the entangled nature of human behaviour: 'people act out in symbolic ways' (Byrne 2016).

The emerging writers whose stories grace this collection engage in the play of symbolic action and detail, capturing sadness and imperfection through an apprehended fictional world—an abstracted reality. The stories resonate because they are intensely focused upon a very particular ontological and epistemological inquiry: Why do the characters in these stories see what they see? How do they know what they know? Perhaps it is *this*—the focus upon a very particular form of sensory apprehension—that lies at the heart of short stories that resonate beyond the final lines of text. Edith Wharton captures this sentiment superbly:

> The impression produced by a landscape, a street or a house should always, to the [writer], be an event in the history of a soul, and the use of the "descriptive passage," and its style, should be determined by the fact that *it must depict only what the intelligence concerned would have noticed, and always in terms within the register of an intelligence.* (Hodgins 2011: 79, my emphasis)

The stories in this collection manage sensory subject matter, as an apprehended reality—focalising the consciousness of a very particular register of intelligence. Certainly, without this degree of focalised specificity, story detail might be nothing more than a shopping list of ideas and observations. As Flannery O'Connor (2006: 524) notes:

> The fiction writer has to realize that he can't create compassion with compassion, or emotion with emotion, or thought with thought. He has

to provide all these things with a body; he has to create a world with weight and intention [...] A story always involves, in a dramatic way, the mystery of personality [...] showing you how some folks *will* do, *will* do in spite of everything. (emphasis in original)

Memorable short stories resonate because they are attentive to specificities and particularities: to detail as it relates to a unique consciousness. This process of transposition underpins the link between concrete and specific detail and metaphorical meaning—it explains how we might read compassion, emotion and thought in interwoven narrative images—newspaper-swaddling and salt-panned rice fields, a tent zipper and a karri forest, stirrups (adjusted) and a light box, a cautiously passed teaspoon and divots in a puddle, methodical hands and synthesised music, seatbelts against bare skin and barbed wire, nails clacking cobblestone and burnished bronze, intricate paper folds and a bamboo forest, a scrunched charcoal skirt and snapped scaffolding, a warm dead body and a bouncing head—in this way, concrete and specific detail is capable of translating the unsayable—in this way these authors approach the incurable imperfection, the sadness, of the present.

Inked by my love for literary realism, or, what I have been lately referring to as a type of abstracted realism, these stories capture a sense of incompleteness through carefully crafted detail—tiny, telling detail. In this way, they exemplify Flannery O'Connor's (2006: 524) deceptively simple claim—fiction must convince through the senses:

Fiction operates through the senses, and I think one reason that people find it so difficult to write stories is that they forget how much time and patience is required to convince through the senses. No reader who doesn't actually experience, who isn't made to feel, the story is going to believe anything the fiction writer merely tells him. The first and most obvious characteristic of fiction is that it deals with reality through what can be seen, heard, smelt, tasted and touched.

I am deeply interested in the realist text as a sensory 'narrative image'. This is what attracted me to the work of the authors in this collection: the deft use of concrete and specific detail. The ways in which the writers utilise sensory data is part of a broader conversation about truth and imagination—at the heart of so much discourse around realist writing.

The relationship between art and life, and by extension realist fiction and reality, is taken up by Victoria Walsh (2009: 236), who notes that Francis Bacon 'remained consistently in sympathy' with Baudelaire, among others—with the belief that 'the purpose of art was not to "illustrate" life but to bring it closer to the imaginative and the sensory'. In this way, Bacon argued, 'a picture should be a re-creation of an event rather than an illustration of an object' (Walsh V 2009: 236). Perhaps most pertinently, Bacon argued that:

> the prerequisite to realizing the full potential of the painted image was its synthesis with the idea which it was seeking to bring into form, ensuring that, as Bacon explained in 1953, 'idea and technique' were inseparable. (Walsh V 2009: 237)

Literary realism merges idea and technique so that they are barely, if at all, distinguishable—technique is masked by writing that seems 'at one' with reality. My use of the term 'abstracted realism' derives from comments made by Michael Meehan: novelist and Professor of Writing and Literature. Meehan suggests, writing that 'feels real' is often:

> beautifully abstracted [...] conveyed through deep subjectivities, with the style shifting as it dramatises the consciousness, the subjectivity of each narrator—'Realism' is of course, always a confidence trick—making the reader feel that these blank marks on the page somehow give us a 'real world'. (Meehan 2018)

How do we navigate the realist text as a narrative image? In my own writing practice, I have agreed to cut, sometimes radically, because in doing so I could more clearly see the architecture that was left standing. In this way I am indebted to editors, to writers and thinkers, who have helped me see my own story 'scaffolding' in a more acute light. This is the tightrope we walk, as we toil with our stories, as we engage with the work of other writers. When is less *more?* When is less *less?*

To interrogate story material in this way is to ask about the relationship between concrete and specific narrative detail, and idea—it is to plot the capacity of language to act as a scaffold for the otherwise irresolvable and unsayable. At the end of a recent mesmerising lecture at Swinburne University, novelist Arnold Zable asked students: 'Do you ever think what you're writing is just weird?' (2018: Guest lecture). 'Go there,' he said, with great conviction, encouraging writing students to push forward, trusting the writing-mind even if the conscious, logical mind is second-guessing—What am I writing? What does it mean? In this, Zable speaks the same language as Bruce Pascoe. 'Tell it true,' says Pascoe, earthed and steadfast (2016: personal correspondence).

Around the time of Zable's lecture, a writing friend wrote to me about the subject matter of his new novel. He said: 'It's about [X] but things are quickly progressing off-piste' (2018: personal email correspondence). This put me in mind of Kafka's version of 'going there', progressing off-piste as a kind of deviation and distraction in the form of apparitions:

> My feeling when I write something that is wrong might be depicted as follows [...] A man stands before two holes in the ground [...] waiting for something that can only rise up out of the hole to the right. Instead, apparitions rise, one after the other, from the left; they try to attract his attention and finally even succeed in covering up the right hand hole. (qtd. in Corngold 1996: 84)

The stories in this collection are testament to each author's diligence in labouring off-piste—going there—paying homage to the incurable imperfection of the present, capturing the unsayable at the level of the sentence through tiny, telling details. Each of the stories is marked by a focalising consciousness that is very thoughtfully rendered: memorable for the use of idiosyncratic voice, and, concrete and specific detail.

As I worked with the authors in this collection—as I thought of Garner and Malcolm, as I contemplated the sadness of the present and the incompleteness of lived experience, as I worked with my own story material—I was in conversation with another writing friend. We discussed the highs and lows of going there and, in particular, the complexity of dark subject matter. I recalled the Raymond Carver story, 'Tell the Women We're Going'. I said: 'Have you read the Carver story about the rape and murder of the young woman?' My writing friend looked at me quizzically and I said: 'Unless I'm misremembering, making up a different version of that story'. In this story, Carver—like Garner and Malcolm—enters into a conversation about the haunting, entangled complexity of human behavior.

The story first appeared in *What We Talk About When We Talk About Love* (Carver 2003: 48-56). Edited by Gordon Lish, the story ends like this: 'He never knew what Jerry wanted. But it started and ended with a rock. Jerry used the same rock on both girls, first on the girl called Sharon and then on the one that was supposed to be Bill's' (Carver 2003: 56). As I re-read this story, I was reeling. It was not the story I remembered.

I reached for *Beginners*. This collection, published nearly three decades later, contains the original, unedited version of 'Tell the Women We're Going', and other stories (Carver 2009: 81-94). In this version, Jerry rapes one of the young women. He prepares to leave her at the site of the rape, in the semi-wilderness. Instead, he apologises. Then he punches the young woman and slams a rock against her face: 'He actually heard her teeth and bones crack, and blood came out between her lips' (ibid: 92). Jerry proceeds to choke the girl but, finding he cannot commit, takes a larger rock and drops it on her face, repeatedly. In this version, the story ends when Bill (a friend of Jerry's) finds him standing over the girl with the rock. The ending reads:

> But Jerry was standing now in front of him, slung loosely in his clothes as though his bones had gone out of him. Bill felt the awful closeness of their two bodies, less than an arm's length between. Then the head came down on Bill's shoulder. He raised his hand, and as if the distance now separating them deserved at least this, he began to pat, to stroke the other, while his own tears broke. (Carver 2009: 94)

How to read this story without weeping, along with Bill? I sobbed outright, but that is hardly the point. What do the two versions, side-by-side, suggest about the perils and possibilities of handling someone else's story material?

My writing friend referred to the edited version of 'Tell the Women We're Going' as, comparatively 'unhinged—psychotic world' (2018: personal correspondence). In this, he highlights the crude manner in which the edited version groups the men together, as a plural unit—a combined 'sinister-ship'. The edited version is nowhere near Carver's deeply probing questions about the complex relationship between the heart and the mind—questions Carver poses in the context of rape, violence and love. Perhaps this deviation from the original is explained by Lish's (2015: 208) admission that he is 'not really interested in anybody else's heart or mind, or even in [his] own'. Carver is undoubtedly deeply interested in questions of the heart and mind, and the riddled intersection between those domains. To my mind, the significance of working with other writers is implicitly tied to the act of acute listening. What sadness of the present is the author contemplating?

Some readers would support the decision to cut the heart-wrenching and haunting details of the rape and murder from the final scenes of 'Tell the Women We're Going'. They might ask: Are the details *necessary*? The answer, to the extent that there is an answer, seems to depend upon what the story is *about*—what sadness of the present, what incurable incompleteness, is Carver grappling with? Did Lish ask? Did Carver quibble? Did Carver agree to cut, but later prevaricate?

William Maxwell, whose editorial style stands in stark contrast to Lish, suggests that:

> real editing means changing as little as possible [...] What you hope is that if a writer reads the story ten years after it is published he will not be aware that anyone has ever touched it. But it takes many years of experience—and love—to be able to do that' (*Paris Review* 1982: 127).

Did Lish love Carver's stories? Did he love them *enough*? In the original version, Carver opens a world for us—pathways to deep and deeply troubling forms of imagining—questions of violence and tenderness—moments of loving tenderness amidst violent atrocity. The edited version of the story limits the reader's ability to enter a conversation about these things, as disturbing as that conversation may be.

Maxwell worked as an editor at the *New Yorker* for many years: like most of us he had a day job outside of writing but, more pertinently, he notes that his writing was necessarily slow due to his uncertainty about the unfolding story. He suggests:

> Undoubtedly, if I knew exactly what I was doing, things would go faster, but if I saw the whole unwritten novel stretching out before me, chapter by chapter, like a landscape, I know I would put it aside in favour of something more uncertain—material that had a natural form that was up to me to discover. (*Paris Review* 1982: 110)

Maxwell (1982: 110, 113) embraces 'uncertainty' as the momentum that drives the writing mind. In doing so, he inadvertently explains why he was celebrated for being such an assiduous editor. As we engage with the work of other writers, we bear witness to the writer's attempt to capture uncertainty, to plot the unsayable. In many instances, we engage with work that is in a state of becoming.

Uncertainty, as it relates to evolving form, is precisely what Flannery O'Connor means when she suggests that 'the more you write, the more you will realise the form is organic [...] it is something that grows out of the material [...] the form of each story is unique' (O'Connor 1984: 528). To listen acutely is to be attentive to the relationship between concrete and sensory detail—it is to be alert to the materiality of form as a representation of an underlying idea.

Maxwell is asked: 'What exactly is the force that makes you a writer?' (*Paris Review* 1982: 113). He suggests: 'Why, what makes anyone a writer—deprivation, of course' (ibid). After completing a hasty draft of this afterword—the ideas plotted here still swimming in my thoughts, I arrived home, present and not present—I opened the laptop, briefly, and in a 'note to self' wrote: *Put in the bit about longing—link to the incurable imperfection of the present and the unsayable.* I remembered *longing* in Maxwell's *deprivation*. To my mind, we are saying the same thing.

What Maxwell calls deprivation, Proust refers to as the imperfection of the present moment—Modjeska recognises herself as a temporiser, while Davies reels in the face of authors capturing the unsayable—Zable implores writers to 'go there' and O'Connor champions sensory detail as a means of 'getting there'—Wharton brings this discussion together within the exquisite terms of a register of intelligence. These thinkers, together with the writers in this collection, take an interest in creative writing as a linguistic bridge between the brain, the heart, and the mind.

This bridge is underpinned by the work of imagination. Maxwell suggests that it is not about 'getting the facts down' but rather 'the degree of imagination you bring to it' (ibid). Maxwell is musing upon the subject of abstracted realism and, in this, he is reminiscent of Francis Bacon (Walsh 2009: 248) who suggests that:

> Real imagination is technical imagination. It is in the ways you think up to bring an event to life again, in the search for the technique to trap the object and given moment [...] Art lies in the constant struggle to come near the sensory side of objects.

To create sensory objects within the context of narrative is to capture meaning metaphorically.

In her Nobel acceptance speech, Toni Morrison untangles the myth of an old woman—blind, renowned for her wisdom. A group of children approach the woman and one of the children asks: 'Is the bird I am holding living or dead?' (Morrison 1993). Reflecting on her writing practice, Morrison suggests that 'speculation on what (other than its own frail body) that bird-in-the-hand might signify has always been attractive to me' (ibid). Morrison speaks to the seductive lure of the signification process—slipping away from 'real' time to a ghostly ether—where the frail bird-in-the-hand takes flight, where 'unmolested language surges toward knowledge' (Morrison 1993). To track the flight of unmolested language is to take an interest in the pathway to the unsayable—to unpick the act of going there, to engage with work that belongs, at least in part, to a primal moment of narrative composition—to handle work that is in a state of becoming.

When we engage with the work of other writers, we enter into an act of acute listening—asking whether the *idea,* as conceived by the author, is exposed in its most acute light. When I introduced Arnold Zable, at the time of his guest lecture, I reflected upon his skill in capturing human brokenness—I praised his aptitude for acute listening. This skill is critical to writing. It also underpins thoughtful engagement with the work of other writers.

In the *ACE Anthology. Arresting, Contemporary stories by Emerging writers*, each story is marked by the urgency of idea, captured as raw sensory data. The stories are authentic, the voices diverse and multi-layered. It has been my privilege and pleasure to listen acutely to these authors, and their stories. I look forward to seeing what these writers will do—will continue to do—translating longing and deprivation, capturing tactile events through a concrete and specific lens, in minutiae.

Works cited

Byrne J 2013 *The Book Club*—'Jennifer Byrne Presents: Books That Changed the World', Volume II, ABC 1.
http://www.abc.net.au/tv/firsttuesday/s3845571.htm#

Carter L 2016, 'Poets on Porches Drinking Tea' in *Meanjin*, Winter 2016, Melbourne University Publishing Limited: Melbourne.
https://meanjin.com.au/essays/poets-on-porches-drinking-tea/

Carver R 2003, 'Tell the Women We're Going' in *What We Talk About When We Talk About Love*, Vintage: London, pp. 48-56.

Carver R 2009, 'Tell the Women We're Going' in *Beginners*, Random House: London, pp. 81-94.

Corngold S 1996 'Kafka's Die Verwandlung: Metamorphosis of the Metaphor' in Corngold S (ed). *Franz Kafka The Metamorphosis,* Norton critical edition, Norton & Co.: New York.

Garner H 2016, 'The Rapture of Firsthand Encounters' in *Everywhere I Look,* TEXT Publishing: Melbourne, pp.181-184.

Hodgins J 2001, *A Passion for Narrative*, Toronto, McClelland and Stewart: Ontario.

Lish G 2015 in 'The Art of Editing No.2', Interview with Gordon Lish by Christian Lorentzen, *Paris Review* (ed. Stein L), Issue 215, Winter 2015.

Maxwell W 1982 in *Paris Review* 1982, 'The Art of Fiction No. 71', Interview with William Maxwell by John Seabrook, *Paris Review* (ed. Plimpton G), Issue 85, Fall 1982.

Meehan M 2018, Keynote Presentation at Swinburne University, June 7 2018.

Modjeska D 2002 'Writing Poppy' in *Timepieces,* Picador: Sydney, pp. 67-94.

Morrison T, Nobel Lecture December 7 1993 in *Nobel Lectures, Literature 1991-1995* (ed. Sture Allén 1997), World Scientific Publishing Co.: Singapore.
http://www.nobelprize.org/nobel_prizes/literature/laureates/1993/morrison-lecture.html

O'Connor F 2006, 'Writing Short Stories' in *Creative Writing: A Workbook with Readings*, Routledge: Oxford.

Walsh V 2009, '... to give the sensation without the boredom of conveyance': *Francis Bacon and the Aesthetic of Ambiguity*, Visual Culture in Britain, 10:3, pp. 235-252.

Zable A 2018, 'The Power of Words', Guest Lecture at Swinburne University, September 2018.

Acknowledgements

I would like to acknowledge the generous support of the Australasian Association of Writing Programs, for contributing to the cost of publishing this anthology.

I would like to thank the Australasian Association of Writing Programs, together with our partner organisations: Australian Short Story Festival, Ubud Writers and Readers Festival, and University of Western Australia Publishing, for unwavering commitment to providing prizes and publication pathways for emerging writers. The authors featured in this collection were identified through these initiatives.

I take this opportunity to thank the 2017 judges of these prizes: Associate Professor Dominique Hecq, Dr Luke Johnson, Professor Michael Meehan, Dr Rachel Robertson, and Dr Anna Solding—for lending their considerable expertise, for insightful and respectful management of submissions.

I would like to thank Shane Strange, publisher: Recent Work Press, for agreeing to publish this anthology and for being 'the real deal'. An extract from the Recent Work Press Website as 'case in point':

> Our authors are our partners. We are careful about selecting the writers we work with. Often they are asked personally to submit work, or to participate in an anthology. We believe in them as writers and artists and we want to share our collaborative success.

Thank you to the authors in this collection—it has been an inordinate privilege and a supreme pleasure to work with each of you, and your ace stories.

Thank you to Ruth Armstrong and Andrew Drummond, for proofreading this anthology with discerning eyes.

Biographies

Supatra Walker is a PhD candidate at the University of Newcastle where her creative thesis and memoir *Luk-krueng—Between Worlds* examines place, identity and belonging from a bi-racial perspective. The eldest of four children born to a New Zealand father and Thai mother, Supatra grew up in Thailand and New Zealand before coming to Australia where she has worked as a governess, camp cook, bookkeeper, jillaroo and school dental therapist in Australia's far north. Since then she has been a farmer, a horticulturalist and herbalist and is passionate about women telling their own stories in their own words.

Joshua Kemp is an author of Australian Gothic and crime fiction. His short stories have appeared in literary journals such as *Overland, Seizure, Tincture* and *Breach*. Last year he won the Australasian Association of Writing Programs (AAWP) Chapter One Prize and is currently halfway through his PhD at Edith Cowan University in Western Australia.

Andrew Drummond is a writer from Melbourne, who also works in education and community mental health. His writing has appeared in *Meniscus, Explore, juice, Rabelais, ars poetica* and a number of anthologies. He is winner of the Australasian Association of Writing Programs / Ubud Writers & Readers Festival Emerging Writers' Prize.

Alison Kelly is an English tutor, short story writer, and an undergraduate student at the University of Newcastle. Alison specialises in English and Ancient History. She lives in Newcastle, in the inner-city, with her partner and cat.

Sue Brennan is a writer of poetry and fiction. She was shortlisted for the Alan Marshall Short Story Award (2016, 2018) and the

Polestar Literary Award (2016). She has had poetry included in the *Poetry D'Amour Anthology* (2016, 2017, 2018). She is currently working on a novel.

Ivana Rnjak is a Serbian-Australian writer and student of Professional Writing and Editing at RMIT. Her writing appears in *Going Down Swinging* and *Unsweetened*. Ivana writes stories that explore belonging, identity and nostalgia. She lives in a big sharehouse somewhere on the 86 line.

Sophie MacNeill is a writer and PhD candidate at Griffith University on the Gold Coast, where she is working on her first novel. Her practice-led research explores transcultural identity in the context of contemporary return narratives. Sophie's short fiction has appeared in *Talent Implied: New Writing from Griffith*, *Pink Cover Zine*, and the *Bareknuckle Poet Annual Anthology*.

Ruth Armstrong has been a General Practitioner and a medical journal editor. She is currently undertaking a Master of Arts in Creative Writing at the University of Technology, Sydney. She writes short fiction that is often travel-themed. 'Paper Cranes' is the winner of the 2017 Australasian Association of Writing Programs / Australian Short Story Festival Emerging Writers' Prize.

Kerrie Knox is mother of three living in Croydon, a leafy outer eastern suburb of Melbourne. She is currently completing a writing unit through Macquarie University. Concentrating mostly on short-form fiction, she is continuing to hone her skills and open herself to various writing opportunities. Two of her short stories have been published in *Short and Twisted*, an anthology of short tales with a twist ending. She is currently working on a collection of short fiction and plotting her first novel.

Lisa Smithies is a writer living in Melbourne. She writes short (and very short) stories and screenplays about science and fiction, but not necessarily in that order. She has a day job as an Emergency Department nurse.

Julia Prendergast is a Lecturer in Writing and Literature at Swinburne University, Melbourne. She is Deputy Chair of the Australasian Association of Writing Programs (AAWP). Julia's most recent short stories feature in *Australian Short Stories 66* (Pascoe Publishing, 2018). Her novel: *The Earth Does Not Get Fat* was published by University of Western Australia Publishing (2018). Julia's short stories have been recognised and published: *Lightship Anthology 2* (UK), Glimmer Train (US), *TEXT* (AU) Séan Ó Faoláin Competition, (IE), *Review of Australian Fiction*, Australian Book Review Elizabeth Jolley Prize, Josephine Ulrick Prize (AU).

2018 Editions
The Uncommon Feast **Eileen Chong**
Inlandia **K A Nelson**
Peripheral Vision **Martin Dolan**
The Love of the Sun **Matt Hetherington**
Moving Targets **Jen Webb**
Things I Have Thought to Tell You Since I Saw You Last **Penelope Layland**
The Many Uses of Mint **Ravi Shankar**
Abstractions **Various**
Ace: Arresting, Contemporary stories from Emerging writers **Various**

2017 Editions
A Song, the World to Come **Miranda Lello**
Cities: Ten Poets, Ten Cities **Various**
The Bulmer Murder **Paul Munden**
Dew and Broken Glass **Penny Drysdale**
Members Only **Melinda Smith** and **Caren Florance**
the future, un-imagine **Angela Gardner** and **Caren Florance**
Proof **Maggie Shapley**
Black Tulips **Moya Pacey**
Soap **Charlotte Guest**
Isolator **Monica Carroll**
Ikaros **Paul Hetherington**
Work & Play **Owen Bullock**

all titles available from
www.recentworkpress.com

RECENT
WORK
PRESS